Bone

and

Jewel
Creatures

Bone

and

Jewel

Creatures

ELIZABETH BEAR

Subterranean Press 2010

First Edition

ISBN
978-1-59606-274-0

Subterranean Press
PO Box 190106
Burton, MI 48519

www.subterraneanpress.com

This book is for Jay.

One

Bijou's fingers angled from her palms as if someone had bent them aside under great heat and pressure. She shuffled about her cavernous, shadowed workshop in parody of a bride's hesitation step. Eighty years a Wizard of Messaline—the city of jackals, the empire of markets—had left their wear.

It was not that she grew frail. She had no opportunity for frailty when her work with forge and hammer, with wire and pliers kept her strong.

But of late all her strength must be bent to shouldering the burden of years before she could take up any other work, and each year was weightier than the last. Still, Bijou did what she did, and not one other alive could do it.

For a decade, Brazen the Enchanter had been pestering her to take another apprentice, someone youthful and broad-backed who could pump the bellows and heave the ingots, who might tend the maggots and the corpse-beetles, who would haul the ashes and stir the porridge. And each time Brazen pushed her, Bijou the Artificer would gesture round the arched spans of her loft. The sweep of her arthritic hand encompassed rustling rafters, the shifting and clattering upon the floor, the bone-tapestried walls between the tall multipaned windows, the serried ranks of dried articulated skeletons laid along her slate-topped benches awaiting the jeweler's art.

"I have all the assistance I need," she would say.

"Even so," Brazen would answer. "Even so."

He was her only frequent visitor. Sometimes Ordinaries came for repairs on their automatons or to purchase a new one, and the mews-man, the newsman, the greengrocer and the butcher and baker and dairyman all made their deliveries, but Bijou was without companionship except for the Enchanter.

Thus, when the string of silver bells over the great double portal jangled without appointment, she suspected who the caller would be. She had been engaged with a hair-fine drill, bringing a thread of platinum between the upper and lower beaks of a raven, so rather than setting her tools down, she turned to Ambrosias, which was directing the lamp.

She told it, "If that is Brazen, see him in. If it is anyone else, please take a card."

Carnelian eyes unblinking in an ivory ferret-skull, Ambrosias humped up its rear end, set the lamp down with such great care Bijou barely heard a click, and scuttled down the leg of the bench to race to the door. Her other creatures made way: Ambrosias was her oldest surviving creation, and though it was but crudely fashioned it held pride of place and seniority. None of the others, even those fifty times its size, dared to challenge the eldest.

Many of the later Artifices modeled upon real creatures, crafted from skeletons. But Bijou had made Ambrosias in mock of a centipede larger than any centipede the waking world had seen. It was three canes in length from pincers to hind-end. Its core was the articulated vertebrae of a horse, its legs the rib bones of cats. The rough-tumbled stones set along its length were agates and jaspers, cheap jewels in crude sand-cast copper settings. The legs on the left side rippled slower than those on the right—a fault Bijou had never quite been able to tune out of it—so if it were not wary, it tended to run in circles.

But for seventy years it had served her loyally, and Bijou trusted it.

The rattle of bony limbs across the marble floor was a ceaseless accompaniment to her work. Now, as Ambrosias reared up by the door, several of its brethren moved curiously from their places. The door-answerers including her newest, giant Hawti with its chased tusks and the enormous belled bangles clashing on each ankle. In Hawti, Bijou's mature prosperity was apparent. Though she had created the elephant Artifice simply because a corpse had become available, and not under commission from any particular client, the surface of the skull was filigreed with gold inlay and emeralds. In each eye socket lay a jewel knobby as Bijou's fist—if Bijou still could make a fist—soaking in the available light. For the right side, she had selected a spinel, darker red than any ruby, and on the left a yellow sapphire, pale as straw.

Hawti paused behind Ambrosias, rocking from foot to foot in anticipation so the bells and bones rang and rattled and the jewels and precious metals trembled with reflections. Ambrosias, more familiar with the infrequent phenomenon of company, simply grasped the view-portal in its bony limbs and drew the metal aside. Well-oiled, the slide did not rasp.

Bijou knew the pattern of the clicks of ferret teeth, the silvery tremolo of the cymbal-coin that depended from a gold band encircling one of Ambrosias' vertebrae. "Brazen?" she asked.

Hawti rattled in the affirmative.

Bijou permitted herself a gusty sigh and set down her drill. "Open the door."

Even half of the giant double portal was too heavy for Ambrosias, but Hawti dragged the left one wide. There are no bones in an elephant's trunk; Hawti's was crafted of a portion of a boa constrictor spine.

It had not always been hard work crossing a level floor, Bijou thought, shaking out her filigree cane. She moved slower now than Lazybones, which crept through the shadows of the rafters on curved claws, sunlight sometimes glinting from the mosaic of glass chips and mirrors mortared to its skull, and never came down at all.

At least she had not succumbed to palsies—there was a little resting tremor, perhaps, but far less than one would have expected for her age—and her mind was sharp. Her work remained.

Palm-sized crab-shell Artifices scurried aside as she shuffled forward on gouty feet. In the rafters, the condor Catherine fanned bony wings stretched across with watered silk and ragged feathers, batting in startlement, shaking its spring until its gears rattled *tic tic tic*. Bijou hushed it, but not before Brazen had walked boldly in between Ambrosias and Hawti, dragging a tall veiled box on a little red wagon behind.

Cold wind blew past him from the gray autumn day outside. Argan and olive leaves scraped across the floor, only distinguishable from the bejeweled crab carapaces by virtue of drabness. But even Bijou's Artifices were drab in comparison to Brazen the Enchanter. He wore velvet trousers, a silk turban, and a smoking jacket resplendent in oranges and greens. A tall, hairy barrel of a man, half Bijou's age, he was already gray-goateed and streaked with gray through the temples and along the part of straight blond hair that swung below his shoulders.

"Brazen," she said with her rusty voice, and teasing, added, "the Shows-Up-Just-In-Time-For-Lunch."

"Bijou," he cried, throwing his arms wide, the handle of the cart still in the left one, "I have brought you an equinox gift!"

Something within the draped box gave forth a rattle.

"Bones," Bijou guessed, which was mostly a safe guess in such cases.

"It's possible," Brazen said, with a wave of dismissal. He turned to drag the pall to the floor, emitting as he did a terrible stench of rot. It didn't trouble Bijou; the work of the corpse-beetles in the back garden smelled far worse.

She limped forward to peer into the box.

Or cage, rather: five feet tall, but no more than three feet by four feet in its footprint, just exactly filling the floor of the little red wagon. And inside the cage, huddled in blankets, a stiff wide collar about its throat of the sort one used to prevent an injured animal from tearing at its wounds, lay a naked child.

"I don't want that," Bijou said. "Who did you buy it from?"

He released his breath slowly, through his nose. "If you can save it, I thought it will be an extra pair of hands. Or hand, anyway."

Bijou stared at him, mutely. He took her arm, though, and led her around the side of the cage, where she could see the injured limb it clutched to its chest. Bijou, with her eye for skeletal structures, could see that the hand had been deformed to begin with, twisted back on itself even worse than her own. It looked as if the child's fingernails had gone untrimmed for a long while and had grown into the flesh of the palm.

The jewel-translucence of fat gleaming maggots ornamented its suppurating wound. "Those are keeping it alive. Or the poison in the wound should have killed it."

"Nature's surgeons," Brazen said.

Bijou snorted. "What's your name, child?"

It huddled deeper in the blankets, eyes shut tight, and made no more speech than an Artifice.

"It doesn't talk," Brazen said. "It is a feral child. If you cannot save it, I thought you could use the bones."

THERE WAS NO saving the hand.

Brazen returned to the great spider-legged steam-carriage he had left crouched in the street on creaking pistons, leaving Bijou alone with the child. While Hawti barred the door, Lazybones dangled Bijou's smock from its enormous hook-hands so Bijou could shrug it on over her robes. She retied her leather apron and obtained Ambrosias' assistance to unbutton thirty-two buttons. Sleeves rolled up, she scrubbed her arms and hands. Bijou was still spry enough to manage this, and she could rely on the strength of her Artifices to restrain the patient.

That the child did not speak came as a relief. Bijou engaged in a certain amount of daily conversation with her Artifices, but they did not answer except in actions. Human voices grated. The child looked about six or seven years of age—though malnutrition could make them seem younger. If it were feral, it had grown beyond the age where it could have learned to speak.

Which meant that Bijou stood no chance of explaining that what she was about to do was for its own good. She would have to minister to it as she would an animal, while defending herself from attack.

Perhaps she should consider ether, but ether was dangerous, and she only knew how to use it to suffocate. She had all the skills necessary to perform the amputation, however, and Ambrosias' deft pinchers would serve to clamp pulsing arteries until Bijou could stitch or cauterize them. She would do it fast.

Beside the slate-topped bench she meant to use as a makeshift surgery, Bijou arranged her tools—the delicate scalpels and the sharp, sharp knives. Ambrosias and some of the others fashioned leather straps with heavy buckles and fastened one to each leg of the table. There was a belt for the child's waist and another for its neck.

They filled the brazier and set it to heat, and so was all laid in readiness.

Hawti, Ambrosias, and Lucy—an Artifice that had started off as the skeleton of a gorilla whose dissected corpse Bijou had purchased from the Zoo of Messaline—approached the feral child's cage. Hawti and Lucy lifted the cage—"Gently, gently!"—down from the wagon and set it on the stone floor of the loft. Within, the child huddled on its blanket, the uninjured hand pressed to the underside of its awkward fanlike collar as if it would have liked to put the fist against its mouth. It made no sound at all, like a tiny woodland kit huddled in shelter, waiting for the danger to pass.

"Shh, shh," Bijou said, soothingly. She hunkered as much as her inflexible spine would allow and peered between the bars. "I'm going to have to hurt you, Poppet. But it will be better after, and what I break I'll mend."

Lucy, bone-and-brazen armature clattering, came forward to block the cage door as Hawti reached to slide the bolts. Catherine spread enormous wings, settling to the roof of the cage with all its jewels casting sparks of amplified light around the room. The child heaved itself to feet and one hand, cramped into the far corner of the cage, plate-matted hair hanging about its face in foul vines. Still, it made no sound, but it dragged the infected hand close up to its breastbone and hunkered, showing bared teeth, wrinkled nose, and slitted eyes.

"Bring it out," Bijou said, and limped away from the cage with her cane rattling on the floor.

Lucy pulled its arms in tight together at the elbows and reached into the cage with giant, gentle hands. Bijou knew the delicacy of Lucy's touch. There was no other among her Artifices that Bijou would trust with fragile porcelain or glass, or the egg-tender skulls of new-hatched songbirds. But Lucy—with bones as thick as a human wrist, and the ropes of baroque peach-colored South Sea pearls dripping from humerus and ulna—could perform all but the finest work.

And now, hopefully, it could catch the child without injuring it.

The cage wasn't deep; the child batted at Lucy's hands, swung its blanket and flailed, but it couldn't keep the Artifice from delicately encircling its scrawny biceps. Once the gorilla's hands were closed, the brazen clockworks inside the chest of the skeleton tick-ticked, and the powerful arms began to bend, drawing the child inexorably from the cage.

Still, it made no sound, but it snapped and twisted in Lucy's grasp as if it were seizing. The lithe body jerked this way and that, thrashing horribly, bruising itself on the cage door. Its working hand lashed out and fastened around an upright, but Lucy continued to move it gently away from the cage and the arm stretched taut, knuckles whitening, elbow extended beyond a straight line as the arm bent back from the shoulder.

"Wait," Bijou said. Lucy paused, angling its greatbrowed head so the lamplight caught a shimmer across cobalt-glass-and-gold eyes. "Ambrosias."

The centipede needed no instructions. It rattled up the bar, levered its leg-ribs under the child's fingers, humped its spine, and pried. Bijou's face scrunched in sympathy as the little thing winced with effort, but its tiny fist was no match.

It kicked out, bare feet drumming against the chest plate that covered some of Lucy's finer machinery, at least one kick hard enough to leave a smear of blood on the rubies and sapphires of her design. "I should wash you first," Bijou said to the child. "But surgery will be enough fear for one day."

Between them, Lucy and Hawti brought the child to the bench, liberated it from the fan collar, and strapped it down. The slate table-top was too hard under the child's skull. Bijou sent Catherine for a blanket. While hand-span crab-Artifices clattered across the floor in swarms, Bijou made a little pillow and a brace to hold its head immobile.

All this work would come to nothing if it dashed out its own brains in panic and pain.

Bijou moved to her tools. "Better if you don't look," she said, and selected a single-edged knife, razor-sharp, as long as the length of her hand.

Despite the maggots, the putrefaction had spread. Crimson strands threading pale flesh showed the advance of septicemia, and the limb felt hot and hard halfway up the forearm. "The elbow, then," Bijou said, with a sense of relief.

It would be easier to disarticulate than the wrist.

The child was still watching, wild-eyed, silent, horrified. Bijou washed her aching hands and the infected arm in alcohol. The child's skin shuddered at the cold, but Bijou was careful not to splash the moonstone-gleaming maggots. They were only doing what they were born for.

Moonstones.

Yes, that should do well.

Bijou folded her crippled hand around the hilt of the knife and nodded Hawti forward to help restrain the arm. "Lucy, give it a scrap of leather to bite on, would you? And when you have done that, please cover its eyes."

She didn't know if it would be easier for the child to bear without watching. But—on the slim chance it might live—it would be better if it didn't associate her with pain.

She set the blade against skin. Now, at last, the child began to scream, as Bijou with her crooked hands drew a slicing line across the back of the joint, so as to leave the great blood vessels intact as long as possible.

THE CHILD QUICKLY lost consciousness, though Bijou completed her work in less than two minutes. Ambrosias humped over the little limp body to pinch arteries tight before she severed them, so while blood was lost, it did not spray violently. White cartilage gleamed smooth and beautiful in the disarticulation, and when Bijou set the knife aside to lift the soldering iron from the brazier the tip glowed an orange almost yellow. The cauterization took an instant. The child never stirred.

Bijou stretched the flap of skin she had left attached at the front of the arm across the stump and stitched it. Then she gave Ambrosias the amputated arm to carry out to the garden.

"Bathe it before it wakes," she said to Catherine and Lucy. "Keep the stump dry."

Catherine, who had been perched on a lamp arm overhanging, rattled the vertebrae of its long neck like a shaken marionette.

The garden smelled faintly of rot and its high walls were well-attended by carrion birds, though none so spectacular in their size as the beast the living Catherine had been. One small bold crow buzzed Bijou's head, cawing, as she crossed to the lidded tray that would hold the child's arm while it decomposed. It was molting, a single feather missing from the left wing. Ambrosias reared up to threaten it, and it flapped back violently, squawking.

Bijou laid the arm on stained loam. No need to add carrion beetles, not when the maggots were already at work. With the bones of the hand deformed and probably fused, redesigning the limb would be challenging.

As she lowered her head to investigate the clawed fingers, something caught her attention. It was the necrosis itself, the bones of the palm clearly visible between busy corpse-worms.

And tucked between them, something that should not be there.

"Ambrosias," Bijou said.

The centipede reared up beside her and poked its ferret-skull head over the edge of the bin. Telescoping feelers made of segmented wire brushed the wound, then pincers slipped forward, between the maggots, and tugged.

A scrap of something soft and pale came free. Bijou lifted her jeweler's monocle to her eye and bent towards it.

Bloodstained and bruised, but what Ambrosias held was a tattered white rose petal.

Two

IN ITS SLEEP, the child jerked and shuddered. Bijou was not surprised that it slept. It had been terrified, badly hurt, and exhausted, and she had no way of knowing for how long it had been ill. The delicate ribs rose taut under tented skin, however, and there had been little flesh over the joint to cut through.

It might sleep the day away and be the better for it. Bijou could use the time to prepare a place.

Her Artifices would perform the hard work, fetching and carrying, scrubbing and hauling, but they must be supervised. Ambrosias, at least, could scuttle up the attic ladder and, with Hawti's assistance, lift down a disassembled bedstead, sheets, feather-beds, feather-pillows, and some of the many tanned pelts stacked there. But as for the rest, well. A corner by the hearth must be cleaned (Lucy did the sweeping, while Lupe lay, silver-and-steel-shod jaw resting on bony paws, and watched with telescope-lens eyes) and the cage brought over and scrubbed shining.

Judging the child by the state of the cage was unfair; there was no telling how long it had been in there. And yet—Bijou leaned with both arms on the handle of her cane. "It's probably not housebroken, is it?" she said idly to Catherine.

Catherine hid its head under a tattered wing.

So there was the bedstead. And there was the cage. And there was access to the side yard, which was high-walled and narrow, and Bijou thought that if the child could not be taught to work the latch, one of the smaller Artifices could be delegated as a door-thing. There remained only the matter of keeping it from worrying its stitches out. Bijou thought she could make a chased leather and metal cuff that would strap into place.

Bathed and rid of the necrosis, the child smelled better. It barely stirred when Lucy tucked it still voiceless into the small bed, where it seemed to find the warmth and softness soothing. It curled tight, pulling all but its now clean and braided hair and the one delicate hand still left to it under the covers. Bijou thought, not unkindly, that her Artifices might seem less terrible to a feral child than to one which suspected their origin.

The damp braid left a water stain on the pillow case. The hair was black, lustrous, the skin—despite the fading summer—brown as toast. It had a child's face, still, with an undeveloped nose and chin, but Bijou thought from the angle of the bones and creased margins of closed eyes—black lashes drawing a smudged sooty line above the cheekbone— that with growth the child would prove some by-blow of the silk-and-spice traders who traveled a long cold road to Messaline each spring and summer, from the farthest East. The mother might have concealed her pregnancy under voluminous robes and given birth squatting in an alley—but how then had the child survived for six or seven years?

It would in any case probably grow up beautiful, if Bijou saw it adequately fed. She wondered if it could be taught to walk upright. She needed to consult her books.

A modicum of research suggested that outcomes were variable. The child was unlikely to learn to speak, or comport itself as befitted a human being. But if its mind were undamaged, it might learn to follow commands, to care for itself, and to perform simple tasks through demonstration. It was, in other words, no different from one of Bijou's bone and jewel creatures, and Bijou thought that she could care for it.

Though what Brazen had been thinking, bringing an injured child to an old woman living alone, she would never know.

As ANTICIPATED, THE child slept the clock around. In the morning, some of Bijou's clients came to make preliminary inspections of the Artifices she was constructing for them. The Young Bey's giant was nearly done, requiring only assembly—which could not be managed here, as Bijou's ceilings were not tall enough—and dressing before its animation. The Bey's man said he would send a send a cart and workman to move the pieces, and Bijou accepted the second third of her payment with graciousness. It had been heavy work—the giant was constructed of the petrified bones of such antediluvian monsters as eroded from the desert mudstones, with the gaps made up in elephant and rhinoceros—and intricate, and Bijou was coming to the opinion that she had not charged enough. But the Bey's man seemed well-pleased, and soon the monumental heap of silk and wire and jewels and skeleton that crouched in one corner of Bijou's loft like a child crammed into a shipping container would be standing guard over the city, banded agate eyes in its enormous horned skull, bony fingers curled about the handle of a spiked club taller than the Bey.

The Bey's man did not mention the bed or the cage in the corner, and the child remained as cannily concealed as a cat for the duration of both his visit and that of old Madam Oshanka, the Northerner, who had come to collect the Artificed skeleton of her small curly dog, which Bijou had re-dressed in its own tanned, grey-muzzled skin.

Lupe had watched the process with suspicious lenses, but once it became evident that the small nervous Artifice was not staying, seemed to have accepted its presence without baring jeweled teeth. Hawti, Bijou suspected, had made something of a game of pretending to be about to step on the darting creature—but Bijou was certain that it was a game, for Hawti was perfectly capable of dodging crabs and kittens made of bone and gemstones and precious metal.

Bijou's Artifices made old Madam Oshanka nervous, which Bijou found ridiculous, considering what she was carrying from Bijou's loft cradled in her arms. But if a little fur and padding and glass eyes made a difference—well, so be it.

Bijou thought of Madam Oshanka as old, but she was ten years younger than Bijou. That didn't seem significant when Madam Oshanka's back was bent like a gaff and her hands shivered with every gesture, and she wore so many coats and rugs that if she had not been attended by her coterie of strong young servants, she would have looked more like a carpet-seller's stall than a great Ordinary lady.

Bijou showed her out and gestured Hawti to bar the door. Restive, clattering, the elephant did so. With relief, Bijou turned back to her loft, a private space once more. Private—except for the bright eyes and strip of forehead that had appeared above the covers on the bed.

The child had awakened calm and free of fever. Its knees were drawn up, a fragile barrier. From the silhouette under the blanket, Bijou could tell it held the stump of its arm pressed hard to the ribcage, but its breath came normally, and it had been sensible enough to get its back to the wall.

It looked like it was going to live. Which meant it was going to need a name. And breakfast.

"Ambrosias," Bijou said, "start the tea." She tromped closer to the bed, waiting for the child to make some sound or begin to withdraw, but it only watched her approach through narrowed eyes. Lupe, which had arrayed itself beside the bed, rose slowly on paws of wired and flexing bone. The child startled.

"Are you hungry?"

The child crouched back, left shoulder raised and forward, chin dropped to the collarbones. Protecting its injured arm and throat. Bijou opened her mouth and touched her toothless gums with callused fingertips. Her paws were nearly as deformed as the one she'd amputated from the child, she thought bitterly. If still more functional.

"Eat," she said. "Hungry?"

Just an animal response, crouched and tense, but she noticed that the child feared Lupe far less than it did Bijou herself.

From the kitchen floated the aromas of stewing couscous and vegetables sautéed in oil with saffron and almonds. The child's head turned. It sniffed deeply and its stomach gave a long, conversational rumble.

"Right," Bijou said. "Eat."

She turned away, trusting that the further smells of cooking would draw the child from its bed.

IT ATE LIKE a mantling falcon, awkwardly crouched over the plate with its left elbow and right stump spread wide and spiky. At first it had just shoved its face into the plate and been shocked to find the food painfully hot, drawing back with a silent frustrated cringe. But it was clever; as soon as it had seen Bijou scooping mouthfuls of couscous onto a bent lime leaf pinched in her cramped hand and blowing on them, it mimicked her actions, shoveling as fast as it could bear, no more chewing its food than would the raptor it resembled. Bijou gummed her own food slowly, appreciating the spices and the aroma of argan oil through dimmed senses.

They sat chewing suspiciously at one another, Bijou settled on fat cushions and the child huddled on the floor, shivering with a chill across its naked shoulders.

Bijou, trying potential names inside her head, wondered if there was any way to convince it to wear clothes. Well, one thing at a time. It was clever. It could learn that warmth and shade were portable.

"Emeraude," she said aloud.

The child cocked its head at her like a listening dog.

"Emeraude," she said, and pushed her half-finished plate towards it across the floor. She had no appetite these years.

It crouched a little lower, suspicious. She nudged the plate again. "Emeraude," she said. "Eat."

The leather-wrapped stump of its right arm squeezed so hard against its brown torso that the flesh paled, but the left arm snaked out long and slid the plate closer.

Not a dog, Bijou decided, watching it.

Something shyer and more fastidious, wilder and even less certain.

A jackal-child of the jackal-city.

THERE'S MORE FOOD here than the cub has ever seen, and no-one is trying to snatch it away. The old creature hurt the cub, before, but the cub barely remembers it except in a haze. Now it brings the cub food and soft things to nest in, and none of the other strange bony creatures seem afraid. So maybe the old creature is not an enemy. It's not very big, anyway, and it moves with deliberation.

There's some other creature in the shadows overhead that does the same thing. The cub can hear it there, the slow click of claws on wood every few heartbeats. It might be one of the bony creatures; everything here that does not smell of food or of the old creature or of chemicals smells dusty, musty, like desert-dried bone.

The wholesome smell of food drives out other considerations. Aromas carried on steam rise as if from the entrails of a fresh kill. But it's hotter than that, hot enough to sear, so the cub crouches over the plate wishing it dared growl and protect its claim.

The fever and dizziness are gone, the wounded useless limb no longer a dragging anchor. There's pain, but it's bearable pain, except the itch of healing. The cub might gnaw at the healing stump, but no matter how it stretches its neck or twists its shoulder, teeth will neither reach the wound nor penetrate the leather.

The brothers-and-sisters could do it, for the teeth of the brothers-and-sisters is sharp. The cub has never been as sharp or strong or deft as the brothers-and-sisters. It can run longer, though, and wear down prey as the brothers-and-sisters cannot.

There is enough food here for all the brothers-and-sisters. The cub should bring some back, except the food is too hot to touch, and too crumbly to carry. It might pack its gullet and then regurgitate, but it doesn't know where the brothers-and-sisters and the mother can be found, or how to find its way back to them even if it did.

So it eats, warily, all that its given, gorging until the skin of its stomach stretches uncomfortably. Then it angles itself out on the cushions, panting, and does not protest—not even a weak whine—when the old creature takes the remains of the food away. The cub is too sleepy and warm to be afraid.

It has to roll to the other side to pillow its head on its foreleg, though. Because the useless one is missing, which is probably why it hurts less now.

WHEN BIJOU HEAVED herself from the nest of cushions, the child was already twitching in dreams. Its resilience amazed her; the strength of animals, not to dwell in *what could have been*. Instead, it adapted, accepted, and carried on.

"Watch it," she said to Catherine and Lazybones, who peered down from the rafters. Lazybones' round glittering head swiveled on the deceptively long neck, bent between strange arms. Light caught on the mirror-encrusted shoulderblades.

The palms of Bijou's hands were still laced with the network of fine scars she'd inflicted upon herself with the mirrors. For all its soft deliberate dignity, Lazybones was not a creature anyone would care to stroke.

The child slept on while Ambrosias clattered close and cleared the plates away, while Bijou stomped to her nearest workbench. There, sealed in a shallow-lidded watchglass, lay the shredded petal, brown and curled at the edges. She sparked the lights over the bench and adjusted the reflectors to send brilliant light showering down.

Jeweler's tweezers and her scalpels would do for the dissection, though she already suspected what she would find. But it was neither scientifically nor sorcerously responsible to assume the accuracy of one's speculations.

Bijou would investigate.

Blinking in the eye-watering light, hands already aching, Bijou selected her tools. "Lupe," she called. The wolf trotted over, toenails and bones clattering on stone. Left-handed, Bijou reached down and smoothed the copper-chased skull. "I need your eyes," she said.

Lupe reared up, front pawbones on the edge of the bench, and cocked her head at the work surface. The light through her lenses coruscated for a moment before it focused, but then Bijou was looking at a much-enlarged projection of the rose fragment on the surface of her work bench. The projection was large enough to show every pore and vein in the petal, and make out a suggestion of the cellular structure.

Delicately, she peeled back layers of tissue, the motions of scalpel and tweezers so tiny she could only see them in magnification.

She found what she was looking for. Between the surfaces of the petal ran tiny threads as pale as moonlight. She scraped them free, returning a few to the watch-glass, and bent close to study the remainder in the projection.

The silky fibers were the protective, venomous spines of a puss moth caterpillar, and they threaded the structure of the petal as if they had grown there.

There was only one gardener in whose garden this poisoned blossom might have grown. Kaulas, the Necromancer.

DAYS PASSED, AND though autumn drew down around the great city of Messaline, Bijou had no occasion to leave her home or her work. As for the child, Emeraude was surprisingly little trouble. It was fastidious, making the enclosed side garden its toilet until Bijou demonstrated the use of the squatting toilet in the rear garden outbuilding. When it saw Bijou bathing in the old tub, it wanted to play as well. Despite the frustrations of teaching it to keep its stump out of the water, it learned quickly, by mimicry, though Bijou at first despaired of making it stand up and go about on its legs. But once she—with Lucy's assistance—taught it to recognize the benefit of wearing clothes against the sun and in the night's chill, it mastered walking erect quickly.

Its bones were clean within a week.

Compost kept the corpse-beetles and blowfly larvae at work in the back garden warm and productive, and Bijou had clay ovens to set about for when the nights—inevitably, though only in the deepest part of winter—might dip towards freezing.

Bijou learned from the bones. As she had suspected, the deformity was not merely the result of an old injury. The bones were warped, and two fingers had had no bones at all. The child had been born with a useless limb, which explained why its mother might have chosen to expose it. How it had survived since was a story about which Bijou could only speculate.

What she could not comprehend was how it had run afoul of Kaulas the Necromancer, and what it might mean that she, Bijou, and Brazen the Enchanter had intervened.

The stitches came out the day after the bones were polished, Emeraude watching curiously while Bijou steadied its arm and Ambrosias snipped and pulled. Emeraude bit its lip once, but remained stoic, and Bijou thought if it could have gotten its head down to the end of its stump it would have licked the blood away.

The next morning, with moonstone and silver and wire, with some of its own bones and some bones that were better, Bijou began building the child an arm.

THE CUB CLIMBS and explores, but it does not try to run. The old creature is gentle and like the mother, bringing food and tending hurts, and it makes a warm soft place for the cub to sleep in. It grumbles to itself and it creaks and lurches when it walks, but the cub is used to old creatures that are cranky. They're sore and no longer strong, the cub knows, and so one pays no mind to their irritability.

And anyway, the garden wall is high for a three-legged cub to get over, at least until the cub is strong again.

But the cub can explore the garden, whose walls bound all sorts of wonders. There are the roses and the palms, the passionflowers now merely huddled vines as winter encroaches. The lemon and lime trees are heavy with fruit in the cold, and once it understands what is wanted, the cub helps the centipede-creature harvest them. It is pleased to help feed the old creature, or, as it is starting to think of it, the old-mother. The limes are stacked in baskets; the lemons salted and packed away in lemon juice to pickle.

Although the old creature makes that attention-noise— "Emeraude!"—to try to stop it, the cub nevertheless bites through the thin skin of one before it is pierced for pickling, and makes a face. This is food. This could be eaten.

But for once in its life, the cub is not hungry enough to eat things that taste bad just because they are food.

There are secrets and lairs and amazing corners within the old creature's den as well. The cub discovers ladders by watching the centipede-creature scurry up and down them, into and out of the rafters. There are creatures that live in the rafters too: there is the vulture-creature with its dusty smelling wings, and there is the slow sparkling creature. The cub clambers up a ladder, balances across the rafters, and touches the slow creature once, but shallow bloody slices across its fingertips convince the cub of the unwisdom of that idea. The cub makes no sound—it knows better; sounds draw attention—but the red dropping from its hand brings the old creature grumbling from whatever it was that the old creature does at its benches, to wash the wound and tuck the cub into bed, on a short leash, for the rest of the day.

After that, the cub is careful not to touch the slow creature.

The slow creature cuts.

But that expedition across the rafters has shown the cub something it did not know existed: a mysterious wooden hatchway.

The cub is *fascinated*.

The next day, when the leash is off, it will climb the ladder again.

IN ALL MESSALINE, there were only three individuals upon whom Brazen the Enchanter would dance attendance. One was the Bey, whose rule Brazen chose to honor because Brazen did not himself care to govern. One was the Ordinary entertainer and famed beauty Madam Incarnadine, his paramour.

And one was Bijou.

Brazen's house was at the bustling heart of the city, halfway up the hill topped by the Bey's palace and gardens. To reach Bijou's loft—which lay on the West bank, surrounded by warehouses and inexpensive apartments—Brazen's carriage scurried effortlessly over swarming streets and marketplaces, and danced across with the broad shallow river with great splashing and no benefit from any of Messaline's four bridges. Spidery elegant legs seemed too frail to bear up the crystal-windowed body; narrow feet thinned to pointed needles. Those rested lightly on the cobbles, dancing between goat-carts, dog-carts, and donkey-carts; litters, rickshaws, bicycles, and flocks...schools... *hordes* of pedestrians; water carriers, pastry peddlers, workmen, marketing women, news-sellers, a few Ordinaries in palanquins. The street society of Messaline.

They scarcely glanced up as the Enchanter's carriage hurtled by surefooted, though a single misstep could have impaled a hapless bystander like an insect on a thorn. The city folk accepted the Wizards as just one more feature of the urban life of Messaline; only tourists cringed.

The carriage never stepped on anyone.

Ragged lines of close-packed tiled roofs—blue, red, orange, ochre—flashed in and out of the sight through crystal ports in the convex belly of the carriage. Chimneys and copper flashing broke the pattern, catching slanted morning light. At street level, Brazen would have been awash in a sea of scents and sounds and textures—the heavy sway of silk, the musk of civet, the cries of birds. The rich savor of grilling lamb, dustiness of mingled spices, sweep of a pigeon's wings as it evaded the net. The shrieks of parrots from four continents and monkeys from three.

Smoke and dust and confusion, but Brazen sailed above it all in the cool clean air of his sealed carriage, an observer from afar. Sometimes he missed the tang of charcoal and piss in the streets. Sometimes. But who needed a Wizard's tower, when you could bring one with you?

This time, Brazen had nothing to transport, and so he did not trouble to kneel the carriage. A rope ladder slithered from the hatchway once he'd drawn to a halt. He scrambled down, hair and bright-striped felt coat flaring in the hot autumn wind that had swept away two weeks of coastal chill, and grounded himself—he thought—half-elegantly. He was expected; Ambrosias awaited him in the street, reared up to head-height. It did not sway as a living creature might, so rather than glittering the jewels along its spine reflected sunlight in steady gleams.

Coat still swirling about his calves, Brazen stopped before the Artifice. It bowed with a measuring tic-tic-tic and the shiner of its cymbal, then swept about, sudden as a mongoose, and led him to the door. Though the massive double doors were closed, the sally-port stood open, guarded by the reclining, watchful skeleton of a wolf. Brazen stepped over Lupe—its tail rattled once on the tile in welcome—and let himself into Bijou's loft.

The Artificer was seated by the fire for once, and Brazen was glad to see it. She didn't rest enough, claiming that soon she would have time enough to rest forever…in the embrace of Kaalha the half-masked.

The old have nothing to pace themselves for, she'd say. This is the final sprint. Run. Run. See how far you can get before you fall.

The cast of her features concerned him as he came to her. It could be hard to read expression on a leathery face marked by years of sun, dark as lava rock beneath the springy gray snakes of her hair. But he had some experience. She did not look in pain, but the lines from nose-corners to mouth-corners had drawn deep and her eyes were hooded.

Brazen stopped before her and hooked a padded stool over with his foot. He dropped down on it, sitting by her feet as of old, though perhaps with greater dignity.

"The child?" he asked, not glancing at the trundle bed and the clean cage standing open not so far away.

"It's in the attic," Bijou said. "I sent Catherine and Lazybones to watch. It should be fine. For a time."

With both hands on the arms of the chair, she heaved herself up. A little rocking was required to get her there, but she did not ask for help, so Brazen did not offer it. He stood, instead, and had the cane he'd made for her so long ago—during his own apprenticeship—shaken out long and ready when she reached for it. "Walk with me," she said.

A painful task, because her dragging steps hurt him. Still, he followed her, a little to the left, as she hobbled toward the benches among the pillars at the back of the hall.

She said, with steely directness, "Where did you find that child?"

"It fetched up," he answered. "The cook has been feeding it on the steps, along with the jackals and the feral cats. When she noticed the thing was injured, she brought it inside. You were the only one who stood a chance of helping it."

"Because I take in strays," she said.

She had turned to him with that comment, a crinkle at the corner of her eye the only clue that her expression teased.

"It wouldn't be the first," he said. "If it's out running around, I imagine you helped?"

"I had to amputate." She lifted her free hand and tugged at the wattle along her throat, as if even slack skin had grown too tight for her. Her cane clicked on the floor, apposite to the shuffle of the foot she dragged. It was twisted almost sideways, now, the striped wool sock and straps of her sandal protruding from under the hem of her robes. She gestured to the nearest workbench. It made his own hands ache, to see how hers were twisted. "There it is."

The bones were clean, bleached pale, though age would eventually mellow them to ivory. Bijou had begun the process of articulating them, of building a working hand from salvaged bits and bobs. Some of the hand bones had been replaced by other stuffs: chips of whittled ivory, a block of richly banded coca-bolo wood, a hinge of silver hung on a steel pin. All around the pieces laid like a jigsaw puzzle on the benchtop were stones, precious and semiprecious jewels. From his apprenticeship, Brazen recognized moonstone and chrysoprase, silken blue and green in their luster. "You're making it a hand. That's kind of you—" Bijou grunted dismissively "—what's this?"

Its surface cool under his fingers, Brazen picked up a lidded watch-glass containing a shred of withered brown.

"The source of the infection," Bijou said. "So tell me, Brazen, again. Why did you bring me a child infected by

Kaulas' necromancy? Surely, you don't expect me to believe it was coincidence."

"Necromancy? On the *living*?"

"Dead tissue is dead tissue," Bijou said. "The wound was packed with puss moth threads and white roses—both poisonous and significantly symbolic, I would say." She lifted the watch glass from his hand and tapped it with a forefinger. "The child would have died, without our intervention. And then it would have been completely under Kaulas's sway, don't you think? Its shade his to command, its corpse his to animate? So—if I assume for the moment that you and he are not allied in some plot far too sinister and complex for my old head to fathom—why would Kaulas, the old bastard, have put that child where we were sure to find it? Why would he have chosen a subject who mattered to your household?"

Brazen lifted a smooth needle-sharp hook on a corrugated handle and stroked the point across the back of his hand, pursing his lips at the prickle. "As a means to bring an agent inside my door, it lacks a little something. Neither of us would be likely to keep a rotting corpse around, and he can't have expected me to bring the child to you for treatment. There are too many variables."

Bijou nodded, a slow oscillation of her head that made her fat oval locks shiver against her shoulders. She set the watchglass down and shifted her cane to her other hand. "You know I do not trust him—"

"My loyalties are not divided, Bijou," Brazen said. "I understand that you have learned well to distrust men, but as you were my teacher, I would not betray you. I swear it by my art."

She reached out, as if absently, and patted his arm. Whatever comfort the gesture brought was swept away by her words.

"I know you're not your father, sweetheart," she said. "Never fear you will be mistaken for him."

Three

THE CUB HEARS voices below. Those man-sounds, the ones they make nearly ceaselessly when they are in one another's company. They argue like pigeons; they cluck and coo. The brothers-and-sisters only talk when it is needful, because sound tells the enemies where you are.

And for the brothers-and-sisters, the city is full of enemies. *We are small*, the cub thinks. Not in words as a man would understand them, because the cub's words are smells and body-posture and small yips and growls and vocalizations (the cub's speech is very handicapped, with its small flat ears and its tailless haunches) but in a wordless understanding. Nearly everything that is not prey—rats, cats, pigeons—is bigger than the brothers-and-sisters.

That is why the brothers-and-sisters scavenge and hide and must be smarter—cannier, slipperier, more subtle—than the men and the dogs and all the big things that would kill them and not even eat them, just leave their bodies in the road. The brothers-and-sisters will eat anything that is food and they are tricky and quick. So they survive.

The cub understands that there's information in the man-sounds, just as there's information in the arguing of pigeons. The cub crouches in the attic, where dim slanting light angles across the cluttered space, limning columns of dust. It cocks an ear and an eye close to a gap in the floorboards, and watches.

It recognizes the other man, the one with the old-creature, and at first draws back in fear. That pale-streaked, broad-shouldered man in the sweeping coat was the one who caged it and who brought it here in the swaying, rattling machine-creature. It smells of oil and ozone. Pain and dislocation: a sharp pang of loss. Where are the brothers-and-sisters?

Could it find them again?

Whatever noises the men are making are friendly noises. Some complicated dialogue seems to be underway, involving the old creature leading the pale-streaked one from place to place around the loft, showing it things on tables and making worried noises, while the pale-streaked creature hovers as if the old one is terribly fragile. It's interesting for a little while, and the cub watches, knees bent up beside its ears, balanced on its toes with its haunches tucked under, in case it has to move in a hurry. It doesn't think there's a threat in the attic, and the winged bone creature has followed it up, so there's someone here who *might* be a packmate. Even if the bone creatures are not the brothers-and-sisters, the cub knows it cannot live without a family.

Life is not safe for a jackal alone.

Light shifts across the attic floor, and eventually the cub grows bored watching the men, and its knees grow sore in that beetly position. It comes up to all three remaining limbs, the hem of its smock twisted around its waist, and scurries off among the crates and heaps and piles of furnishings.

There is a great deal here worth exploring. Mice, everywhere, which—if you are quiet and quick—you can kill with a blow of your paw and eat in two bites, pausing between to flick the intestines out, though the fur is not pleasant to swallow. The winged bone creature sees what the cub is doing, though, and after a few moments it too is killing mice with aimed snaps of its sharply curved beak. It does not eat them, though, but tosses them to the cub.

So maybe the winged bone creature *is* a packmate.

There are lots of mice. The cub is stuffed to belly-rounding in less time than it spent watching the men make noises at each other, and still mice flock away every time it lifts a corner of a rug or shifts a crate aside. There is so much food here; the cub has not been hungry since it came. Not once, not even for a minute. There is *always* food.

The brothers-and-sisters should know about this place. Licking blood from its lips, the cub plans.

Replete, it remains more curious than sleepy, and it wonders what other treasures may be up here. Furs and blankets that smell of camphor and make the cub sneeze. Piles of bones—too dry for gnawing, though: these have had all the flavor bleached out of them. All those things in crates. Enticing.

Mostly, the lids on the crates are nailed down, and though the cub pries at them with long fingernails, they will not lift. The mice have taken refuge inside some crates. The cub can hear them rustling.

Rustling is irresistible.

One crate has a lid that shifts easily, and the cub pushes it aside—then dances back, startled, at the clatter as it tumbles to the floor. From below, the old creature makes the attention-noise, and the cub pauses. It crosses the light-dappled floor toward the hatch in a crabwise scuttle, raising more dust, and pokes its face down into the space below.

Both men are looking up. The old creature makes a gesture with its paw, and a questioning noise, so the cub blinks back reassurance—an eye-squeeze and a drawing-taut of the lips, not enough to be a snarl. The cub isn't sure what the next noise means, but it's not a summoning—it has learned the summoning already, because the summoning often means food, or it means that the cub was about to do something the old creature thinks might hurt, and the old creature is often right about that—and so the cub pulls its face up through the hatch and goes back to the mysterious crate, enticingly open now.

The mice, of course, have moved on. The cub isn't hungry anyway, though, so that's all right. It draws its knees up under the smock for warmth and crouches on the edge of the crate, which seems sturdy enough to bear its weight. The stump, it uses for support and balance. The remaining hand is crusty with dried mouse-blood, as is the cub's face, but it knows the old creature and the bone creatures will bathe it when it comes down. This is another reason the cub thinks this might be a pack; the brothers-and-sisters bathed with tongues and teeth, but here, also, the creatures clean each other. The cub thinks when it is a little braver, it might sit behind the old creature and go through its matted fur for ticks and lice. The old creature might like that.

One-handed, the cub picks through the contents of the wooden box. Some are silky-soft; some are fine-furred like pups. There is a curved thing, round and stiff and wrinkled, but made of a cloth with a texture like mole's fuzzy skin. It's decorated with feathers and a cloth ribbon, and a thing like a beetle, but made of shiny stones and metal, and a thing like a flower, except made of sewn-up cloth. The cub strokes the thing and sniffs it—mouse and dust, and the memory of flowers and civet. A hat. It must be a hat. There's more under it: coats and dresses as short against the cub's body as the smock the old creature has wrapped it in. Scarves. A bundle of dried flowers tied at the stem with a ribbon. Vials, some half-full of an amber fluid which the cub can smell through the stoppers. Those make it sneeze even harder than the dust.

At the bottom of the pile is a square hard thing that smells of wood pulp and dye.

A rustle and clatter in the rafters draws the cub's attention upwards, but it's just the mirrored creature making its deliberate way across the rafters. It pauses over the cub, a little to the right so the cub has to lean left when it locks the three meathook claws on each hind leg around the crossbar and lowers itself with meticulous grace to look over the cub's shoulder. The cub turns, surprised when the mirrored creature rotates its upside-down head on the bony neck and looks right back. The shape of the skull and the mirrors make it seem to have more of a face than the other bone creatures, and the old creature has given it a black enamel nose.

Very delicately, it stretches its neck out and touches the cub's nose with its own. The cub holds still—it does not wish for any more cuts from the slow creature's mirrors— but when the slow creature pulls back, the cub reaches out and brushes the three dull but fiercely hooked claws on its long awkward forelimb in return.

They stare at one another for a moment, and then the bone creature makes a strange bob of its head, like a man, and the cub goes back to the contents of the box.

And the hard rectangular object.

The cub has to experiment before it understands how to lever up one side of the top cover and reveal the contents, but when it does it finds inside stiff pieces of yellowed card, woven together at one side with ribbons that also bind the covers on. On each leaf are pasted more stiff rectangles of paper with patterns of grey and black upon them.

They smell delicious, and the cub touches the corner of one with its tongue.

Salty, slightly sweet. Not bad, but the cub is still stuffed full of mice. There is something about the patterns on the cards, that it isn't understanding, and that makes it look harder. It bends its head closer to the book, closing first one eye and then the other.

They are shapes. Flat shapes like real things, tiny and perfectly detailed. Enchanted, the cub balances the open book upon its thighs and turns pages slowly, examining each card in turn. A man looks out from several, male (the cub thinks, from the coats) and pale-skinned and young and tall—even for a man—and wearing hats that make it seem even taller. Sometimes it is with a darker, raptor-faced man in heavy brocade coats and embroidered trousers, dripping with bullion. In others, there is a round-cheeked willowy man, a female, whose dark hair spikes in short locks from under a series of elaborate hats, and whose skin is only a little lighter than and just as satiny-looking as the black velvet of its dresses.

The dresses in this crate, maybe. Or some of them. And the beads and hats as well.

The cub turns more leaves, and there are more images. The same three men, and now a fourth one—another female man, this one unlike any the cub has seen before. Its hair in the images is as pale as the rough-surfaced substance of the leaves. It wears dresses too, beaded and glittering ones cropped short to show long legs. It shows bared teeth boldly, wearing tiny shoes like hooves with a strap over the instep. When all four men stand together, it and the other female man stand at the center, arms around each other, leaning close.

Slowly, the cub puts the book down, open to a image of the first male and the female man embracing one another. It picks up a long coil of beads and lets them run between its fingers like tears, like stones.

Slowly, twist by twist, it winds the necklace around the stump of its left arm.

MOTHS CAME INTO the studio each night, drawn by Bijou's work lights. They fluttered among the benches and beneath the high dark ceilings. Some beat themselves to rags against incandescent bulbs, and some immolated themselves in the fire. The remainder, in morning's drowsiness, came to rest on the walls, where they made a pattern in white and brown, like embossed paper only more beautiful.

Scraping across the workspace in the early morning, when grayness just began to filter in from the garden windows and the stones underfoot were slick with dew, Bijou found them bemusing. Moths were sacred to Kaalha, lady of mirrors, lady of masks. But what sort of goddess blessed an animal so drawn to the light that it would annihilate itself to obtain it?

Bijou crouched painfully to poke up the fire and feed the coals with scraps of kindling. Lucy could have done the tending, but it was Bijou's ritual, and she was loathe to relinquish it. Age had not yet defeated her on all fronts, though it was a war of attrition she knew she was fated to lose. As the flames licked around paper-dry reeds, she wondered—if it was so, that Kaalha blessed the moths in their suicide—which of the four Great Gods or all the myriad little ones was it to whom men were sacred?

Heresy, of course. But she was Bijou the Artificer, and while she did not doubt the gods existed, she also thought it likely they had far more sense of humor than the mirthlessness of stern priests would indicate. She had met the Young Bey, and the Old Bey before him she had known very well. She understood that the hierarchy of officials and functionaries did not always reflect the opinions or personality of the one who sat at their titular head. Wouldn't it be a burden to be a god, and saddled with the upkeep of a cadre of pea-counters and chalice-polishers?

Warmth spilled across the floor. The child, in the trundle bed beside the hearth, raised its head. "Shh, Emeraude," Bijou said, and smoothed tangled hair from its brow with a knotted hand. The cold got into her joints of a morning. She felt it all the way to her elbows. But somebody was either going to have to comb the plate mats out of the child's slick black hair or shave it. Bijou's hair would mat in long tidy springs, and she had worn it that way since she first walked out of the desert dust and into the still-dusty streets of Messaline.

She had been young and straight-spined then, a girl with the height of adulthood but still the body of a boy, and she had walked twelve hundred miles—the length of the River from its headwaters in the mountains where she was born—to come to the legended city.

The city had teemed with donkeys and camels, litter-bearers and sedan chairs and watersellers, and the first bicycles and tintypes had come in while she was still an itinerant magician, making tiny mouse-bone charms for forsaken wives and jeweled bands for forsaking husbands. There had been no airships in those days, no desert-walkers. No electric carts or autorickshaws in the streets. But there had been the father of the Bey, a ne'er-do-well younger son when they met.

And there had been Kaulas, the Necromancer, as young and beautiful as she.

The child had not snuggled back down into its pillow, and Bijou reached gently to tug the blankets higher about its fragile collarbones. But it caught her wrist with its remaining hand and held on lightly. The trembling must be emotion, for it could not be from effort, but it was enough to make the long strings of pearls rattle on its wrist.

Lips pressed tight enough that Bijou glimpsed the outline of teeth behind them, it made a small, hollow, questioning sound. The first sound Bijou had ever heard it make, and she wondered if that were an indication of growing trust, or of extremity.

She knew what boxes it had been in; knew the moment it came down the ladder festooned in swags of black and copper pearls she had never had the heart to Artifice. Too much coincidence.

Perhaps the feral child had a Flair. And perhaps the dawn and moonset goddess had sent the child to Bijou, as surely as she had once sent Bijou to Kaulas. Unless that had been Kaulas's god, red Rakasha, tiger-god of hunger and pestilence and searing summer, of death.

It was said there was no coincidence in Messaline, where the four gods made their homes. Part of surviving—of thriving—as a Wizard was being aware of the patterns of intention upon which the city hung.

Moths were sacred to Kaalha. Even the puss-moths, with their terrible venomed threads. Maggots were sacred to Kaalha, too, as were the scarabs and the shining bottle-green blowflies that birthed them; she was the goddess of transformations and borderlines, after all, and the transformation of old death to new life was the most profound transformation of all.

"Tea, Emeraude, if you are not sleeping?" Bijou reached to pull the weighty iron kettle from the hook, but the child kept its grip on her wrist, so her gesture only served to tug it upright in the bed. "You may keep the pearls?"

She hadn't meant to phrase it as a question, but she wasn't sure if that was what the child was asking, and the child's black-brown eyes were so wide open, pushing with frustrated questions, that Bijou couldn't look away.

The stare held until, in a gesture of profound frustration as eloquent as a cat's, the child lightly dropped Bijou's wrist. It stood, bare feet arching and curling on the cold damp floor, and reached past her to lift the kettle. The weight surprised it; Bijou could tell by the startled glance and the way it dragged the child's shoulder down. The child's strength in turn surprised Bijou, because although it staggered and listed, it did not drop the kettle. It turned, hugging the cast iron against its left hip, and struggled toward the garden door.

Thoughtfully gumming her lower lip, Bijou let it go. Feral children were not supposed to adapt so quickly to human care. They could not learn speech, and they could not learn to tolerate human society, or so it was supposed. Although Bijou suspected many of them were mind-hurt, too simple even for household tasks and abandoned by their parents when it became evident that they would never speak or reason or perform their family duties. Whereas the deformity leading to this child's abandonment was apparent, and physical.

As was the sharpness of the mind behind its earnest, hopeful eyes. And its desire to be of use. When it came back with the kettle dripping water, it bent double under the weight, nearly dragging it, and moving slowly enough that Bijou met it closer to the door than not. She might be old, but her work kept her strong, and she lifted the kettle easily from the child's grasp.

"Thank you, Emeraude," she said, when the child looked up at her with eyebrows arched in canine worry. *Jackal-child*, Bijou thought, not for the last time. Should it have a Flair, after all, how to determine what it might be? How to encourage it?

Why had this child been brought to Wizards—to Brazen and Bijou, no less, Wizards of machines and the dead—rather than one of Kaalha's priests, if the moth-goddess, mirror-goddess wished it saved?

The child scampered back toward the garden while Bijou arranged the kettle over the flames. A moment later, the rapid patter of footsteps brought her around again. The child came trotting, something fluttering black offered in its upraised hand. Even across the loft, Bijou could smell the rot on it. She would have thought the child had retrieved a corpse from one of the composting trays, but Bijou had placed no ravens in to rot in recent days. "Did you find something dead in the garden, Emeraude?"

But it was not dead, Bijou saw—and even a Wizard could feel a little horror when the tragic thing stirred faintly, head questing blindly, weakly, across the child's flat palm. Perhaps the child wanted Bijou to help it, but the bird was beyond aiding. It squirmed with those fat iridescent maggots, the eyes already consumed in the sunken face. A lot of decomposition in such cool weather, when Bijou was as certain as she could be that it had not been in the garden when she had gone out the evening before to make her devotions to the setting moon.

Careful of the grasping beak—too weak to do much damage, anyway—she lifted the bird from the child's palm, leaving a maggot or two behind. As automatically as one of Brazen's Automatons, the child popped the grubs into its mouth and bit down with satisfaction. Jackals would eat anything, and Bijou had consumed her share of raw and roasted insects in her own long lonely walk from the mountains. She did not wince.

She spread the bird's wings, and found what she was looking for.

The suppurating wound, dried pus caked in the feathers about it, at the joint of the left wing and the body. The bird in its final illness could no more have flown than the child could.

Someone had thrown it over the garden wall.

And the wound was packed with flower petals.

"Thank you," Bijou said, and hooked her cane over her arm so she could break the poor thing's neck with her thumbs. A quick satisfying *pop*, and it was dead at last, slack in her hands. Bijou stumped toward the garden and the composting boxes. She'd write to Brazen when that was done.

"Come along, Emeraude. You need to wash your hands before breakfast."

WHILE IT IS true that notoriety offers certain benefits, it is not by any means confirmed that those benefits compensate for the disadvantages. Or, to put it more succinctly, Brazen found it nearly impossible to move unremarked about his city, as he might have in younger and less infamous years. His flamboyance could be concealed, of course—to be taken off again was half its purpose—and his long fair hair wrapped under a turban. His bulk and breadth—his pale skin and eyes—those were harder to disguise.

But an inquest into the surreptitious doings of Kaulas the Necromancer was more than could be asked of a functionary, and so Brazen tugged a cloth cap tight over his twisted-up hair while his turban soaked. He drew the wet white fabric from its basin and wrung it out. One end in his teeth, he made two wraps around his head for the underturban, which would cool him when the autumn sun mounted. Though they moved from the killing summer, Rakasha's season, into autumn—a time of birth and rebirth—still the noontime sun was a danger to the unwary, and Brazen knew he had grown soft in the decades since his own time on the streets.

But the knowledge never left one.

The overturban was double-width, three yards in length, a cool blue gauze the air would flow through. Once he had tucked in the trailing ends of the turban, he folded, stretched, and rolled the overturban, using the knob on a chest of drawers as an anchor. He could have asked his valet to tie it for him, but a professional's touch would show. The man whose persona he was assuming might keep body servants, but a classically trained valet would not be on his list of priorities.

Brazen wrapped his own turban, five wraps, and smoothed the sharp parallel lines with an ivory paper knife to make them crisp. He was out of practice; it took three tries to make the pinch in the center fall even. Still, he thought, examining his reflection—full-face and profile—it would do.

The coat he had chosen was nothing like his usual cut velvet or silk in gaudy bird-bright colors. Rather, he shrugged into ankle-long linen, striped from collar to hem in sand and taupe. Dark brown yarn had been picked through the open weave with a darning needle, leaving the woven-in lines defined with dots and dashes.

Brazen removed his wrist chronometer—his own manufacture, and unmistakable—balanced spectacles he was usually too vain to wear outside the lab on his nose, and stroked his chin in the mirror. It would be better if he had time to grow a beard beyond his tidy goatee, but even so his fair skin would stand out far more than shaven cheeks.

He grunted at his reflection.

It would suffice.

Nevertheless, he slipped a pistol into his sash at the back and hooked a heavy dagger by his right hand. He exited by the servant's entrance, slipping out in company of the greengrocer's wagon. He walked alongside in socks and sandals, swinging his staff with each jaunty stride.

This time, he was not insulated. The scent and the swirl of the streets rose with every turn of the cartwheels, every puff of dust from beneath his feet. Intoxicated, Brazen shrugged wide his arms and drew a deep breath: dung and spices and gutter-reek. Hens fluttered scolding from before a donkey's hooves, one startling Brazen to amused outcry when it ricocheted from his knees and hurtled, shrieking, into an alley narrower than the span of his arms, where it bounced from wall to wall screaming outrage to any who would hear it. The ravens squatting opportunistically along a nearby roofline answered with harsh choruses of laughter, and the jackals slipping like black-backed shadows along the great stone blocks of leaning foundation walls.

Even so early, the streets were full to bruising. Brazen's size gave him some advantage with the crowds; he had his father's height and broader shoulders and towered over most of Messaline's population like a medieval siege engine approaching the walls of a city. Still, elderly market women everywhere were notorious for the sharpness of their elbows.

When seeking information, it was traditional to entertain taverns. And Brazen fully intended to pass through one or two as the afternoon wore by. However, one did not become a Wizard of Messaline without a certain number of favors owed and held and traded, and it was those debts which he first meant to address.

First, in the marketplace, where Isaak the news-seller sat cobbler-fashion on a striped rug beneath a garden-patterned awning, the horny soles of his feet upturned on thighs like ropes of noodle dough. The water-pipe beside him bubbled softly as Isaak drew a taste of tobacco sweet with intoxicating herbs and let it trickle across his ochre-stained moustache. On one corner of his rug, red and yellow thorn-flowers grew in a copper pot, already blooming in celebration of approaching winter.

Brazen crouched in the sideways shade of the awning, one hand still upraised on the balancing staff, and tried to give no sign of how his knees protested. "Isaak," he said, when the news-seller's eyes swung to focus on him. "A word for an old friend?"

Isaak offered him the mouthpiece of the water pipe, and Brazen refused it with a gesture. "Thank you, no."

Eyebrows rose, but the mouthpiece of the pipe went to its hook, and Isaak lifted his coin bowl. "What do you want, Michael?"

The simplicity of Brazen's long-forsaken human name reassured him that Isaak had, in a moment, apprehended the circumstances and chosen to play along. "Carrion," he said, pitching his voice low. "Pestilence. Things that rot before they're dead. What do you know about them?"

Isaak rattled his bowl in answer.

Smiling, Brazen dropped in two of the Bey's silver coins and one of his self-minted gold ones.

"Carrion," Isaak answered, making the gold and one of the silver coins vanish up his sleeve. "You needn't look far in Messaline to find that. It's the city of jackals, Michael. The city of crows. There's carrion on every corner, and heads nailed over every gate."

"That's nothing new." Brazen settled an elbow on his knee, hunkering comfortably. "And *news* is what I'm paying for."

Isaak made a flicking motion with his fingers, as if brushing away flies beside his turbaned head. "Maybe a bit more by way of...direction?"

Brazen glanced left, over his shoulder, aware how fugitive he must seem. But surely any number of those who visited a news-seller had reason to appear furtive. "After all," he mocked gently, "how do we learn news for the selling if not from our earlier clients?"

Isaak reached for the mouthpiece of the hookah and tongued it thoughtfully. He shrugged, a broad fluid gesture that brought one shoulder up to almost brush his ear and rolled the other back in sympathy. "Even my perspicacity has limits, effendi. A little assistance is all I ask. You have, after all—" that same shrug in reverse "—already paid."

The coins meant nothing to Brazen. But on his honor as a Messaline, he would get what he bargained for. "The Artificer," he said. "Myself. Someone is sending us foul little gifts, courtesy of Kaulas the Necromancer or someone who can mimic his work. We are curious to uncover who is employing him."

"Is he necessarily employed?"

Brazen's spanned fingers tapped his knee lightly, the other hand still resting high on his staff. "It does seem likely. Unless he's tossing us gangrene cases and stinking corpse-birds out of sheer Wizardly fellow feeling."

"One would think the Artificer would find a stinking corpse-bird homely and comforting." Isaak let the smoke pool behind his teeth. It dripped over his lips when he spoke. The heady scent alone was enough to make Brazen's eyes water. "Here's a bit of news, then, that might interest you. The Necromancer—all the jackals of Messaline have a taste for carrion. The street dead have a manner of finding their way to his door." He raised his chin, tilting his head consideringly up at Brazen. "The ones no one is willing to pay to have decently exposed, anyway."

Messaline's dead, the ones with someone to care what became of them, were brought with great ceremony to high towers a mile or so from the city walls, and there laid out for the condors and vultures to feast.

"The ones that don't find their way into jackals and feral pigs, anyway," Brazen said comfortably. "So has the procession of corpses stepped up? Tapered off?"

"No." Isaak drew smoke again, tasted it, held it deep, and let it roll off his tongue. "But now, he shops for animals as well. And I have heard from witnesses that his men go among the poorest of the city's poor, the curs and vagabonds, soliciting for employment. Offering…a great deal of money. And perhaps this summer there seem to be fewer street urchins than in the last."

"Is this rumor?" Brazen asked. "Or is it fact?"

"I know a stonemason, ruined by drink," Isaak said. He eyed the mouthpiece of the pipe thoughtfully, and hung it up again. "Who came back out of the Necromancer's employ ruined in the lungs and eyes, as well. He didn't live a month after."

"No one said anything?"

"Wizards," Isaak said. "Who are you going to complain to? And when he died, well, a little man came around to ask if the widow would sell his body to the Necromancer."

"Of course she did." Brazen stood, the prop of the staff welcome assistance. His knees minded the standing more than the crouching, which always struck him as perverse.

"Babies matter more than bodies," Isaak agreed. "And babies are costly to feed."

Brazen nodded. "How much more gold not to share the news of what I asked for, and who was asking?"

"No charge," Isaak said. "That, I do for a friend."

"And the information?"

The final silver coin vanished from Isaak's bowl, proof of a transaction concluded. "Business," he said, and held the mouthpiece out to Brazen again.

Brazen accepted, and sealed the deal in smoke.

THE CHILD HAD its own bed, but most mornings now Bijou awoke with the small thing curled upon her arm. Either that, or with the child burrowing in her covers, hungry and dawn-alert. This morning was no different, and by the time they were fed and the tea was steeping, Brazen had arrived at the door, bearing news and bread from his own kitchen.

Food nor company much delayed work, in Bijou's house. While Brazen watched her, Bijou bent wire. The cool tick of the dark variegated pearls the child had pulled from the attic was soothing; she stroked them, rolling their faint grittiness under her fingertips.

The armature was almost complete. With meticulous attention, Bijou had taken the clean bones and capped the ends in silver, chased each in filigree, and hinged them strongly. Articulating the hand and fingers was more challenging; the bones needed to roll and flex complexly. But the hand of a person was not so different from Lucy's hand—or foot for that matter—and Bijou had made more complicated things.

While Brazen told her what he had deduced of Kaulas's new activities, Bijou hunched over her bench, checking the knots on each silk-strung pearl, lifting moonstone and chrysoprase in jeweler's tweezers and setting them along the back of each finger so they glittered like stacked rings. She thought the child might wear a glove on the hand, eventually, if it wished to conceal the prosthesis.

Or, if it did wind up a Wizard, folk expected stranger things of those than a jeweled skeleton-hand.

"However," Brazen concluded, "none of this explains why Kaulas might go to such lengths to make certain you and I get involved. Because I'm as certain as I have ever been of anything that he sent your new apprentice"—Bijou snorted—"to my door so that I would discover what he was about. Although I flatter myself that I might have noticed eventually."

It occurred to Bijou, as she brushed adhesive deep within a setting, that she was taking on a responsibility she might not live to see complete. Her experience of children suggested that they had a tendency to grow. A prosthesis designed from the bones of a six-year-old would be of no use to the same child at fifteen.

"You are going to have to make the next one for it," she said to Brazen, without lifting her head. A snake-lock fell across her face; she stuffed it behind an ear and idly scratched her arm where the skin was dry and ashy. Palm oil tonight; she would slather herself in it, then scrape it off with the wooden paddle.

"Excuse me?" he said.

"The next arm." Her gesture took in the structure laid out on the table before her. "You are going to have to construct it. You can't take in a stray and then abandon it. It's a betrayal of trust. Once you claim a thing, it's yours."

"But—" He gestured at her, at the bed by the fire, the unused cage with the door standing open.

Now she did turn to him, pulling her shoulders back as far as they would go against the hunch of her collapsing spine. Bijou had seen enough skeletons to have an idea what the bones looked like under the skin. What a pity she could not cut herself open, she thought, and wire in an armature to replace crumbling bone. She could build a trunk for Hawti—the elephant stood now, idly poking the fire before laying more fuel on the coals—but her own body's failures were beyond her to repair.

"Brazen," she said, "I'm not going to be here."

He framed the denial, but he was a Wizard, and you did not become a Wizard of Messaline by denying hard truth. She saw him choose to nod and accept what she had said. *All there is or will ever be,* she thought. *It won't be so long until it's you bidding the next generation farewell. This is your student, not mine.*

Yes, that was it. She rubbed aching hands and said it. "This is your student, not mine. I've done my raising up a Wizard. I've given my heir to the world. Emeraude is yours."

His eyebrows rose. "A crippled feral who cannot speak?"

"The son of the man who betrayed me?"

"Ouch," he said, elaborately. "No son by any means but blood, I assure you. I would be my mother's child if I could be anything, though I never knew her."

Bijou smiled, both because she saw the pang as he experienced it, and because she missed his mother as well. "I forgive you. But the child is yours. When the time comes for an heir, Brazen, we take what the gods provide. There are no coincidences in the city of jackals."

"Which brings us back to Kaulas, and what he wants from us."

"Oh, that's obvious," Bijou said. She bent the prongs down over the final stone, and nudged it to see if it rattled. The cement had set; she thought it would stand up even to a child's antics.

"Obvious?" Brazen rose from the low sling chair he had been occupying, and came to stand beside her. Towering over her, honestly, but head bowed and curiously diffident. Of course he had brought her the hurt thing he found, she thought, with a roll of affection. He would think she could fix anything.

It would break her heart to disabuse him.

"Emeraude!" Bijou called, tipping her head away from the Enchanter at her shoulder. He was taller, and her voice was feeble with age, but it was still impolite to shout in someone's ear.

"What's obvious, Bijou?"

The patter of bare feet heralded the child's arrival at a lunge. Its face and hand were smeared with the composted and irrigated earth of the garden. Bijou decided she would be just as happy not to know what it had found to eat.

Her own jackal years might be too far behind her after all.

The child skittered to a halt beside her and dropped to a crouch at her feet. Both submissive, and out of easy reach for an old woman. Oh, yes, the little thing was cunning.

"What he's always wanted," she said. "Our attention. Kaulas wants us to come to him," she said. "He's baiting us along his trail of crumbs. I'm sure puss-moth is not the only venom he has to induce necrosis, but moths are sacred to Kaalha, and the lady of moths is the goddess I follow, as much as I follow any goddess at all. He knows that; he knows she brought me safe across the desert. So he sends you a child as a message to me, which tells me both that he means to exploit our relationship with each other, and that he hasn't forgiven either you or I for walking away from him."

Brazen wore an expression she knew of old, a line between the brows, one corner of his mouth curled up into the sandy fringe of his moustache. It boded ill for whoever had put it there. "So do we give the old bastard what he wants?"

"Oh, I think if he wants us that badly, he can come to us," Bijou said. She clucked to the child. "Come, stand up, Emeraude. I have a pretty toy for you to try."

Four

*I*T CLICKS. OVER and over, with every tiny movement, every breath, every shift of weight. It's a working hand, with working fingers, no heavier than the real dead arm it replaces, deft and quick. All the cub can think of is the fingers. The fingers that move, quick and fluid, that grasp whatever the cub wishes grasped, that grab and turn and rotate from the wrist to take hold anywhere.

It's a hand.

And the old creature has given it to the cub.

There's no mistake about the gift; the cub knows diffidence, the sidelong glances that one offers to see if the present has been accepted. If the alliance has been forged.

I offer you something of value to show you that I will sacrifice to make you part of my pack. You bring value; I offer value to acknowledge that. We will be a team.

It knows from the brothers-and-sisters how this works, how the offer of a gift leads to cooperation and shared labor. The food wasn't a gift, not in the same way. The food was charity.

But the old creature is shy about the arm, and that means it's an offering.

It clicks. It sparkles. It rattles. Very faintly, but too much noise to hunt with. Which means the old creature does not think the cub will need to hunt, because the old creature is clever and would have thought of that. And so many of the old creature's pack are decorated, noisy, strung with sparkles, ringing with bells.

They are a strong pack. They do not skulk; they parade like lions, like returning warriors.

The cub wants to be a part of this pack. It sits at the old creature's feet as the old creature and the pale-streaked creature talk, and it holds the arm to its chest and rocks on its haunches. Its eyes sting.

Every so often the old creature reaches down to stroke the cub's hair and ears. The other cubs never had weak eyes that watered in pain, or in pleasure. Only this cub. The cub won't whimper, but the tears leak down its cheeks in slow parades.

It could have a place in this pack.

It *has* a place in this pack.

But it has a pack already, and the brothers-and-sisters are somewhere out there.

There is only one solution that the cub can determine. And so, that night, when the old creature snores heavily in its warm, draped alcove, the cub eases from its bed, slides the warm covers taut as the old creature has showed it, and slowly, with great care for silence, pulls the pin with its left hand, removes the new arm from its stump, and lays it out across the bed.

There. No-one would leave such a gift behind if they did not intend to return for it. It's a cache, and a cache in the territory of the cub's new pack. The old creature and the bone creatures will know that the cub is not going far, and that it will be back soon to rejoin them.

Overhead, the slow rattle of the slow-creature's claws among the rafters is the only sound. Even the crab-artifices and the brooch-spiders make no sound in the midnight and chill, though they leave dark tracks stirred through the dew on the floors. As the cub passes toward the side door, the enormous bone-creature with the snake on its face reaches out and strokes the cub's hair.

The cub slips into the side garden, and from there, over the wall.

BIJOU WOKE NATURALLY, a little after sunrise, that small habit already grown foreign. For a moment she stretched, wondering why the child had not arrived to burrow her out from under the covers, demanding breakfast like a cat. Then, painfully, with Lucy's assistance, she commenced the elaborate feat of rising from her bed.

The chill morning had dewed the loft, but early heat was already drying the stones. Still, enough water remained that Bijou's feet and robes smeared a trail behind her. When she pushed the drapes aside and stepped from her sleeping alcove, she noticed at once a similar trail left by the child.

And the inexpertly-made bed, and the object glittering upon it.

Leaning on her cane, hips and knees grinding with morning stiffness that lasted into the evening now, Bijou hobbled towards the hearth and the child's bed. The arm lay across the covers at a perfect right-angle to the bedstead, precise as if measured. Hawti hulked in the shadows by the fire where the gray morning light did not yet reach, bone and metal limned dying red by the faint glow of banked coals. It seemed impossible that such a vast creature could huddle into such a miserable small bundle.

"It's all right," Bijou said, patting the giant Artifice on one sharp-slanted shoulderblade. "It's not in the garden, is it?"

Hawti rocked from leg to leg, disconsolate, and Bijou thought if it had the power, it would be keening. "Shhh," Bijou said. She stumped around the bed once, but did not touch the jeweled arm that lay, pale and hurtful, in the shallow morning light. She followed the trail into the side-garden, and there found the bent stems of rose brambles, a little blood and hair and some fibers from the child's smock caught among the thorns. She would not have thought anyone could climb them.

She had underestimated people before.

As she leaned upon her cane with both hands, waiting for direct sun to creep over the wall and warm her hair, Bijou considered. One possibility was that the child served Kaulas and that it had returned to him. But if that were so, there was no reason for it to leave behind the arm. To obtain a sample of Bijou's best and current work could only serve the Necromancer. True, Bijou might be able to trace the Artifice—but Kaulas had to assume that Bijou knew where he lived.

The child could not speak, unless it had somehow been ensorceled to silence—and Bijou comforted herself that she retained a good understanding of the limits of Kaulas's powers. She did not think it likely. And what good was a spy who could make no report?

The sun had not reached her yet, but the spatter of tiny moving reflections among the curl-leafed but November-blooming roses told her it had painted the top of the arched doorway and that Lazybones hung from its hooks just within, watching over her. Or, at least, watching over her shoulder.

She was fond of the sloth, an exotic skeleton brought back for her from a distant land. It had not proven any usefulness, unlike Lucy or Catherine or Lupe or Hawti—or Ambrosias, first and most loved of her creatures still—but it moved with such meticulous precision, and it glittered so in the light, and it always seemed so *interested* in anything that might be going on.

She turned to look and it lowered itself like a geared Automaton from the rafters, dangling from awkward-jointed legs until its foreclaws swung low enough to brush

Bijou's head, if she had walked under it. It reached out a claw; she extended her hand in turn, brushing knuckles against its hooks.

It was also possible that the child had been meant to serve as a distraction, to keep Brazen and herself occupied while Kaulas carried out his plan. That seemed likelier.

A distraction. A diversion.

Or a test.

What would Bijou and Brazen do, when confronted with his handiwork? How would they react?

Of what were they capable?

In the back garden, something rattled hard, like a mallet thumping the lid of a box. Bijou startled, back protesting as she jerked upright. Lazybones began the incremental process of winching itself back into the rafters, and she hurried under—what passed for her hurrying, now, which might also explain the sense of kinship she felt with Lazybones. The scrape of her feet across the floor, the thump of her cane—she moved a little faster than the mirrored, rattling animal in the rafters, but not by much, and never so gracefully.

She did not need to command her Artifices when she moved with such intention towards an unidentified sound. Ambrosias scurried before her, rib-legs clattering like the rhythm sticks of her childhood. The flapping shadow of Catherine's broad wings passed over, and Bijou could almost feel the shift in the earth underfoot as Lupe, Lucy, and Hawti came along behind, single-file to pass through the ranks of work benches and then fanning out behind and alongside.

In the garden, the birds that sang and quarreled by the pedestal bath went still and crouched in the shadow of Catherine's wings. The condor flew only ponderously without an updraft, but the heavy struggling passage of its wings was enough to bear it to the back garden wall. It landed on outstretched talons and turned heavily, waddling, to face the inside court again. Ambrosias was almost as swift, racing up the wall beside the composting boxes and clinging there, curved and then straight like an osteoid glyph of the letter *kha*.

The hammering—frantic staccato flurries, now, separated by brief listening pauses—came from inside the box into which Bijou had placed the dead crow. "Hawti," Bijou said, taking a step back.

The Artifice reached a boa-constrictor-spine trunk over Bijou's shoulder, pendant teardrop pearls and glittering marcasites sliding cool over skin as they brushed her neck. Gently, in a gap between noises, the tip of the trunk nudged the latch on the box open, and lifted up the lid.

A stench and a bundle of flailing black plumage burst from the box, shedding feathers and globs of rotten meat. The dead bird beat for altitude, a blur of frenetic activity, rising to the top of the garden wall while Bijou was still staggering a half-step that might have landed her, seriously injured, on her back if Lucy had not caught her in a bony arm and steadied her against a massive shoulder. Bijou squeaked, a shrill girl's noise, absolutely undignified in a ninety-six-year-old Wizard.

The dead bird bobbed on the air for an instant, as if seeking a direction, and then Catherine struck from off the wall, falling upon the smaller creature like a stone hurled from a siege engine. The silk-and-feather wings of the condor Artifice snapped on the air like shaken dresses, and both birds hit the ground beside the path in a tangle of beaks and plumage.

Catherine's talons were not made for clutching or tearing. Its skeleton was that of a carrion-eater, adapted for soft, rotten meat. But that was what the raven had become, after all, and Catherine's weight and the reach of its long neck were more than enough to pin it though it still struggled and cursed.

"Ambrosias, a cage," Bijou said. The centipede came down from the wall like a cascade of dice, clattering and rattling, and swept past her ankles. It must have had to venture the attic, because it was the better part of a quarter-hour before it returned, the brass-barred cage—as wide in each direction as the length of Bijou's cane—dragged behind and striking sparks off the slates. Lucy went and took it, then set it beside the raven.

Between them, they managed to get the stinking thing into the cage, where it sulked and rattled its beak on the bars and glared at them from squirming sockets. It reeked of the grave, corpse-liquor dripping from the ragged holes in its ribcage.

Bijou, who was accustomed to dead things, nonetheless shuddered. Catherine scraped its beak and talons clean in the earth beside the path.

"Lupe, Catherine," Bijou said, "watch the dead bird. Don't let it escape."

Lupe gnashed its teeth and sparked the lenses of its eyes, and Bijou answered with a gentle hand across the jeweled skull. "Thank you," she said, and went to send a message.

THE CUB SLINKS through darkness undetected. The *human* city is still at this hour, but that does not mean that the city itself is at all sleeping. This is the hour of the rat, of the jackal, of the moth—of all the life whose city it also is, all the creatures who share these spaces and hollows, these stone and mud-brick walls, these dew-slicked streets that echo with the drip-drip-drip of precious water into cisterns and catchments.

The wings of bats are near-silent, but they silhouette against the night—or against the windows the bats some-times flock around, if the inhabitant sits late with a candle burning to draw the moths. The feet of jackals and cats are near-silent too, but the cub has nothing to fear from jackals and cats. Not so, the dogs that roam the night city in packs, kings of the street. Even a grown male human could find those dangerous: they have been known to break into homes, to pull down vagrants in the street. Beggars fend them away with fire: the brothers-and-sisters must use craft, the art of not being where the dogs are.

The cub is versed in those arts, and moves through the street as silently as the rats do, slinking beside thick walls that may break its silhouette. Its heart hammers sharply, breath low and quick, mouth open to amplify any sounds or smells in the chambers of its skull. Skulk, and slip, and stay alive. That is what the brothers-and-sisters are for. Moving through the cracks and connections, slipping from place to place unseen, with their black backs and their ticked tawny-gray flanks and their twig-slender limbs.

The night city smells of many things—rising bread, rotting meat, sewage, roses, winter jasmine, cold ashes, warm smoke, humans coupling in their dens. The pattern of smells is a map that draws the cub home to its own territory, to the territory of the brothers-and-sisters, all across the breadth of the city.

At the river, the cub pauses. It has not passed the river before. There are bridges, narrow, just wide enough for a rickshaw or two pedestrians, with a low lip on either side but no rail. Not that a rail would matter to the cub, for when it steps on the marble paving stones—Messaline is a limestone and marble city, which in a wetter climate would slowly melt—it hears the echo of its step bounce back from the moving water.

It skips a step back, stops, crouches. The whine rises in its throat but is not vocalized. Things that make noise get found, and things that get found get eaten.

The wind blows from across the river, bringing familiar smells of the pack's territory. Safety. Home.

The cub sets its forelimb upon the bridge, and waits to be bitten. When no teeth snap, it edges forward. One more step. Both hindlimbs. The echoes shatter under its feet, and it pauses, confused again. It can feel its pulse in its eyes, thumping under its jaw below the ear, and it knows that anyone who cares to look can see it easily here, shuddering and exposed.

It must cross. Either walk, or swim.

Humans walk across these things. It can smell their feet, and even the feet of dogs and horses. And other jackals, though none recently.

A scurrying rat bustles past, intent on its own business, disregarding the cub. Good food, if you can catch them, but the rat seems unconcerned by the cub's nearness. Perhaps it can sense the cub's fear and confusion.

If a rat can cross a bridge, so can the cub.

The cub rises from its huddle and scurries—head down, back arched, scrambling on all limbs, just like the rat with one less appendage to work with—across the bridge, sliding on dew down the far slope and crashing against the wall of some human's den at the bottom. A thump, too much noise, and the cub picks itself up, bruised, and makes itself scarce up the hill, toward the familiar smells.

It has passed through this part of the city before, though only with great haste and caution. The brothers-and-sisters are not the only jackal pack, and others do not tolerate trespassers. Because the cub is unlike the brothers-and-sisters—deformed, mangy, pale—other packs may not recognize it as an interloper. But that's a safety the cub would prefer not to rely on.

Here the cub is familiar with the smells, and it knows how the smells have changed. And there is one new smell in particular, overlaying everything, that makes that silent whine bubble up its throat again. It is the smell of the dying raven the cub found in the old creature's den, the smell of the dying limb that the old creature cut from the living cub, so as to make the cub better. And it's everywhere.

Here a bat flutters past, trailing a ribbon of putrescence. There, a limping cat turns baleful eyes upon the cub, but they do not reflect the light from a nearby window. They are slick and luminescent with rot, and in their sockets the glossy soybean heads of carrion worms nod on pale bodies. Around the corner lies a derelict man, from whose pallet the other beggars have withdrawn in horror, moving their shared brazier and their fragile circle of self-protection seven or ten canes distant. The man lifts its head when the cub passes, its sunken cheeks decaying over the remains of yellowed teeth. It makes no sound, and no further gesture, the blank face only swiveling to follow the cub's path.

The cub trots faster, to outrace the sun.

IN THE RISING heat of her garden, Bijou boiled the raven. At first, it struggled in the pot, but the lid—with Lucy's hand upon it—was too heavy for the dead bird to shift. At last simmering quieted the thrashing, and Bijou was left with a cloying stench of rot that adhered in her hair and nostrils and hung about her clothes like a pall. She cast frankincense and dragonsblood into the fire, which at least overlaid the scent, if it did not manage to dull it.

In the afternoon, when the sun was high, she and Lucy poured the broth through a strainer, and pulled the bones one by one from the mess of dead maggots and cooked, fetid meat. Bijou much preferred to work with insect-picked and air-dried skeletons—boiling softened the bones—but there was not time to do this the right way. And she wasn't sure if an undead bird would ever properly rot. Under the Necromancer's power, it might continue in its animate and moldering state until the end of the world.

She was laying out minute bones on the dark gray surface of her work table—sorting meticulously to be certain she had not missed any, while Ambrosias picked through the vile sludge one last time in search of the tiny hyoid apparatus—when Brazen finally arrived. Hawti admitted him at the front door, and he walked in with his handkerchief clutched across his nose. "Vajhir's sacred testicles," he said though muffling cloth. "What *died* in here?"

"This," Bijou said, standing aside so he could see the damp, fragile skeleton. "The forge is heated, Enchanter. Go to it. We have work, you and I."

He turned to obey her, but paused. "Where's Emeraude?"

"Run off," Bijou said, without looking up.

She could still tell when Brazen bit his lip in distress. "I am sorry."

Bijou shrugged, and now she turned to meet his eyes. "She left the arm. Either she'll be back or she won't." When he stood with hands twisted in his coat, stricken, she turned back to her bones and said, "The forge, Brazen. I mean to finish this by nightfall."

BRAZEN HAD NEVER seen Bijou work like this before. She was by habit meticulous, even fussy, precise and exacting and insistent upon everything done and done again until it was done just right, and she had imparted those standards upon him. Today was different. She hammered with swift, measured blows, rough shapes only, crude and effective. Metal bent to her whim. The stones she set were mismatched. She warped bones to fit them into metal, careless of the shape nature had intended. Though she cursed her own errors, they did not slow her.

She was as good as her vow. Sunset smeared the west when she was done. She had jointed and hinged the raven skeleton with tin and pewter, spotted it with moldy-looking agates, sewn a silken cover for the wings and stitched bedraggled feathers along it. She had given it a needle for a tongue, hollow steel salvaged from an ornate, antique hypodermic. She had seated a single fingernail-big flawed sapphire in one eye socket with a glob of solder, so the light caught on the milky fracture plane and made the raven look not merely one-eyed, but cataract-blind.

She would not show it—spine stiff, chin firm—but Brazen could see by the way Bijou shifted her weight that she had burned her strength entire to get it done. He steadied Bijou's paper-frail shoulders as she braced herself with both hands against the bench edge and blew across the raven's nostrils. "Aladdin," she said. "That is your name."

A silent moment, and then a scritching sound. The Artifice thrashed, beat awkward wings, and somehow flipped itself onto its belly. It lay there, keel pressed to the slate, neck stretched out before as if for the chopping block. In the mismatched feathers—some pigeon, some crow—Brazen could see a trembling.

Slowly, it raised its tiny skull, and turned to look at Bijou with the sapphire of its single eye. It opened wide its beak, displaying the silver needle of its tongue, and tossed its head. When no sound followed, it cocked its head from side to side, surprised by what it wasn't hearing.

"I'm sorry," Bijou said. "No voice. I can give you bells or cymbals later, if you want them. So you can make some noise."

Tentatively, Brazen's hand on her wrist as if he could somehow snatch her out of danger faster than she could manage herself, Bijou offered the Artifice her finger. It nipped, but gently, and ran its beak along the surface of her skin as if to lay flat the feathers she did not have. Preening.

When Brazen glanced at Bijou, he saw that a smile cracked her face. "The meat may be yours, Kaulas," she said, rich with satisfaction. "But the bones are mine."

Bijou carried the raven outside, its pewter-shod claws pricking the edge of her hand. Brazen walked beside her, supporting her with a hand on her elbow. *We claim the dignity of age*, she thought, *but the truth is, age leaves us without any dignity at all.*

"My house would be safer," Brazen said.

"Let an old woman die in her home."

He shook her elbow, gently. "Nobody's dying except for *him*."

Bijou looked across the dead bird's back to him, giving the raven a stroke with her fingers to settle the plumage when it cocked its head. "He wouldn't come to your house."

"And he'll come to yours?"

Bijou bent down to whisper in the spaces of the raven's skull. "Go to Kaulas the Necromancer," she said. "And bring him here to me."

The raven twisted its skull on the bones of its neck, casting a cloudy blue reflection across Bijou's cheek. It cawed silently and flapped its wings as if testing their strength. It paused, hopped a step, and flapped again. Two beats, three—it sprang up airborne, wobbled, shed a feather that swirled on the downdraft, and arrowed for the garden door.

Bijou stood, arms crossed, and watched after it until Brazen cleared his throat beside her shoulder.

"Bijou. You said he'll come to your house but not mine? Why do you think so? He's gone to such great lengths to attract our attention, and neither of us would go to him."

"Because he hates me more," she said, and shook the raven into the air. "That's what all the baiting is about. He'll come expecting a fight, you know."

"He'll get one," Brazen answered, and for a moment, Bijou wondered if he knew how exactly he sounded like an actor declaiming on a stage.

"HE'S NOT COMING," Brazen said, at sunrise, in the voice of someone who was only stating a truth long-held to be evident. Jeweled snail-shells crawled on tongues of rubberized silk along the floor. One edged along the sole of his boot. Gently, he nudged it aside. "We need a better plan."

"We need a plan at all," Bijou said. "Bracing Kaulas in his own lair would be foolish. We could bring it to the Bey—"

"And wait six months while his advisors argue over whether to offer us a couple of dozen men, most of whom will desert before they face a Wizard?"

"There is that," she answered, with the complacency of age. "Perhaps rather than merely sending challenges to Kaulas, we need to inconvenience him. Thwart his plot."

"And his plot is?"

She rested a warm hand on his shoulder. "Spreading corruption. He's building an army of corpses. What do you do with an army?"

A rhetorical question, which Brazen answered anyway. "Revolution. If we could convince the Bey that Kaulas has designs upon his title—"

"Still six months with the advisors," Bijou said. "Kaulas could have every man, woman, and child in Messaline rotting under his control by then. We don't know what the plague is, or what spreads it."

"But we know how to stop it," Brazen said, with a sidelong glance at the silver arm still laid across the child's empty bed.

"Yes," said Brazen. "Amputate. Bijou..."

Silently, she stared her answer.

"If we are to make our stand here, then I am staying. Let me send for servants. And for some of my materials."

The stare never wavered. But she licked sunken lips and nodded. "You may."

BY *SERVANTS*, APPARENTLY what Brazen meant was seven *kapikulu*—door slaves, literally; in practical terms these were scimitar-armed religious ascetics, devout followers of Vajhir who had sworn their lives to military perfection. They wore skirted coats of powder blue, buttoned down the fronts with bone buttons. They wore their heads shaved and their eyes hooded under tall crimson fezzes. They came into Bijou's loft, nodded to her as lady of the house, laid pallets with military exactitude along the wall away from the fire, and settled in, two by each door and the seventh patrolling, so silently and with such reserved decorum that Bijou might have mistaken them for statues—for Brazen's creations—if she had not seen them take their places.

"Who's going to feed them?" Bijou asked.

"I'll have dinner sent from the house," Brazen answered. "I have more sweeping the streets for those who show signs of Kaulas' tender medicating. What they find they will bring here."

Unsatisfied, Bijou crossed her arms over her breast. It wasn't cold—the fire was high, and the sun climbing to zenith. She felt a chill anyway. Hawti's silver bells tinkled in the garden. Lupe stayed pressed close to Bijou's calf. The *kapikulu* did not seem to mind them, which made a certain amount of sense for guardsmen accustomed to living in Brazen's house. At least Bijou's Artifices, unlike Brazen's, had no general tendency to explode.

Brazen's servants and apprentices—Bijou honestly could not tell them apart—continued to come and go in the carriage, carting in armloads of chests and caskets and crates, stacking them every which way about the garden and the loft.

"You'll be sorry if those get rained on," Bijou said, following an ant-line of steamer trunks through her downstairs with her chin.

"It won't rain until Winter," Brazen reminded her.

She snorted. It never did.

Five

I N THE HEIGHT of the day, when—even in Autumn—the streets were rather empty, a scrambling in the side yard pivoted the *kapikulu* by that door on their stacked boot-heels and sent them reaching for their scimitars. Bijou tried to surge to her feet, but old bones and slack muscles could not manage; she rocked back onto her camel-saddle stool with a thump. Brazen rose beside her on the instant; she heard one of the *kapikulu* order someone to remain still, and silence in return, except the noise of leaves rustling.

That silence told Bijou everything. "Stop them!" she said to Brazen, low and pleading, and then called— "Emeraude! I'm coming!"

Brazen leaped toward the door, crying "Don't *hurt* it!" while Bijou rocked back and then forward on her camel-saddle, building momentum to thrust herself to her feet. She got her feet under her, whining low at the pain of her gout. She shuffled to the door behind Brazen, swinging her cane, puffed-out ankles protesting every step so she muttered the pain under her breath—*ow, ow, ow*—but kept coming.

The *kapikulu* had charged into the side garden and across its narrow width. They stood against the roses on the far side, scimitars extended and crossed to make a bridge of blades. Or perhaps a barrier of blades, because the scimitars served to block the child from climbing higher.

It seemed uninjured, except the thorn-scratches in its palm and arm, but it had frozen wide-eyed against the rose canes and seemed to be wishing it could melt into the coarse-grained pink granite of the wall. Bijou let go a shaky breath, and clucked her tongue. "Emeraude."

It stared at her as if it were a physical effort to drag its dilated eyes from the sun-stroked blades—stared at her as if it could stare through her, in fact. And then, face contracting in a wince, it uncurled the clenched fingers, dropped from among the rose canes, and bolted across the grass to throw itself into Bijou's robes.

"Shh." Bijou stroked its matted hair, and barricaded it against her with the stem of her cane. "Shh, shh."

It didn't weep, and it stayed silent as the grave, as always, but the weary strength with which it hugged her legs surprised her. As did the abruptness with which it pulled back, and then scampered between her and Brazen, running on all three limbs to the front door. Uncertainly, the *kapikulu* stationed there looked to Bijou rather than stopping it, thought it scrabbled at the bar.

"Emeraude," Bijou said, "wait. *Wait,* child."

The child was not quite frantic. It listened, or if it didn't listen, at least it paused, though its small hand stayed clutched on the bar. Bijou was struck by that hand, by the delicacy of it, the way the skin stretched taut over bones and tendons defined as if carved in yellow ivory. Her own must have been that way once, if a darker version. Bijou shuffled faster, her robes sweeping abound her, brushing the legs of a pair of benches as she sailed between them. The floor bruised the soles of her feet, pressing retained fluid out of turgid flesh, and her cane thumped a hard staccato on the stones.

Of course Brazen overtook her. And without a glance for permission, gently pushed the child aside—it bared teeth at him, but did not slap or snap or struggle—and closed callused hands as unlike the child's as hands could be upon the bar.

"And if it's Kaulas'?" Bijou said.

"Do you think it is?"

Bijou looked at the child and gummed her lip, thinking of the way it had shivered under her touch. "No," she said. She went to the child and held its shoulder to restrain it.

Brazen stepped back with the bar in his hands and let the *kapikulu* crack the door. The child, as Bijou had anticipated, strained toward it, and Bijou tightened her grip and crooned, "Shhh. Shh." She turned her head and called, "Lupe! Hawti!"

The rustle of bells and the tick of bone and metal told her they were coming.

Brazen, flanked by one of the *kapikulu*, leaned into the gap of the just-opened door.

"What do you see?" Bijou asked.

"Nothing," he said. "My carriage. The street." He looked up, and side to side, maintaining cover. It would be a difficult shot, with rifle or with bow and arrow. But a difficult shot was not impossible.

"Brazen," Bijou said, calmly, "I cannot replace you."

"Of course," he said, and leaned back out of the gap, flattening his back against the wall beside the door. A *kapikulu* rested one hand on the door-pull, and maintained a position as sentry. "What do we do?"

Bijou looked down at the child, thinner than when it had left, fine bones sharp through the fragile skin of its face.

She lifted her hand. "Let it go."

The child jumped as if shocked at the release of pressure, and glanced up at Bijou in amazement. "You didn't come tearing back in here just to get the door open," Bijou said. "You want to bring in a friend who can't get over the wall, right? Well, go get them."

She would never know how much of that speech the child understood—none of it, if she had to guess—but it must have grasped the tone of warm encouragement. It hared forward, head ducked, eeling through the narrow crack, and vanishing in a patter of running feet just as Hawti and Lupe reached Bijou.

Bijou closed her eyes—despite all age had robbed her of, her ears were perfect still—and a moment later, heard the feet returning, slower now and heavier, as if the child were burdened. The sentry *kapikulu* jerked the door wider, still blocking it with his foot at a little more than the width of a body. The child staggered through, clutching something against its chest, cradled close in the undamaged arm and stabilized by the stump. A dog?

A *jackal.*

Bijou was reaching for it when the stench hit her, a reek as strong as when Brazen had first brought the child. "Emeraude."

The child didn't answer, but it turned to her, sagging to its knees in a slow-motion collapse until it lay the jackal on the floor and slid its hand out from under. Bijou crouched across from it, the animal sprawled glassy-eyed between them, and said, "Brazen, get Emeraude its arm, please?"

Silent as the child, he turned with short, thoughtful steps and went to the bed. He brought Bijou the child's prosthesis.

Bijou extended it to the child.

There was no staring moment of doubt: the child only grabbed the arm and slid its stump gratefully into the cuff, tightening the buckles with its teeth and setting in the pin. It shook the arm, as if to seat it properly, and Bijou heard the bony fingers rattle, the stones clack against stones. And then the child reached out, right-handed, and took Bijou's wrist and pulled her hand to the wound in the jackal's agouti flank.

"Hold its head, Emeraude," Bijou said. "I don't want to get bitten."

The child furrowed its brow, head cocked like a confused but urgently listening dog. Bijou gently shook its hand from her wrist and pointed to the jackal's head. "Hold the head down. Brazen, get its feet, please?"

Brazen's actions seemed to give the child the clue it needed to follow Bijou's instructions. Gently, crooning—a sound new as the first sound in the world when it fell from the child's throat—the child laid its artifice hand upon the jackal's neck below the ears and pressed down with all its little weight.

Bijou sent Lucy for cloths and hot water and began to clean the wound.

Hard experience told Bijou what she would find when she parted the jackal's pelt. The flesh was hot and inflamed, slick with the infection, and when she smoothed a wet cloth across it the fur came away in crusted tufts. The wound was ragged, scoured by maggots. "Oh, child," Bijou said. "I don't know what we're going to do for your friend."

"Sir," said the sentry, and then waited for Brazen to acknowledge him before continuing, "there's about six more of them in the street. With puppies."

Bijou glanced at the child, but the child had eyes only for the jackal. "By all means," Bijou said. "Show them in."

The wound was nowhere Bijou could amputate, and so Bijou had Brazen lift the jackal to one of her work benches

while its packmates skulked in alcoves and
and flitted behind lawn furniture in the back a
dens. While the child soothed the animal and ı
Lucy helped restrain it, Bijou debrided the wou.
ing maggots and flower petals in shallow bowls 1   .
sorting. She hated to waste good maggots.

It was better than it could have been. Other than in the
immediate vicinity of the injury, the flesh was cool, and
the maggots had nibbled uninfected muscle clean in the
deepest parts of the injury. Under all the rot was something
she had half-expected; a silver pellet with a soldered seam
around the middle, imbedded deep in the muscle tissue. She
set that aside in a dish, separate from the maggots and the
puss-moth threads and flower petals. She would deal with
it in a moment.

For now, Bijou peeled back necrotic tissue around
the edges and irrigated the wound with spirits of wine,
which made the jackal shriek and snap and thrash, and the
child—whose hands, bone and flesh, were full of struggling
animal—stare up at Bijou's face worriedly.

But that was all it took. All she could do, other than
packing the wound with spiderwebs and honey and ban-
daging it with clean boiled cloth. "We're lucky," Bijou said.
"It was a fresh infection. But I don't know if that got it
out." She glanced at the hearth, at the fire.

She didn't say, *we should burn it out.* But Brazen nodded.
"We can give it opium first. If that would make it easier."

"Thank you," Bijou said. "And if that's not enough
either?"

"We have a cage," Brazen reminded, jerking his chin towards the wheeled apparatus the child had arrived in.

"To keep it quiet and away from the others," Bijou said. "So we have half a chance of keeping its bandages on."

"And so if it wakes up dead tomorrow morning, there's a chance of it not flying at the throat of the first one of us it sees. Do you supposed the infection is spread by biting?"

"Like hydrophobia?" Bijou laid her tools across the bottom of an iron pot, for boiling. "No. Every sufferer we have seen has had the same foreign matter in the infected wounds. He is doing this himself. And then sending us the afflicted."

"So we'll know he's coming for us," Brazen said. He shrugged, streaked locks moving over his gaudily-clad shoulders. "Why now?"

Bijou, having known the Necromancer very well, once upon a time, sucked her gums and said, "Fetch me my fine-tipped pliers and the snips, please, Brazen?"

It was decades since he had been her apprentice, but her tools still hung in the same place. In some cases, they were the same tools. He was back in only moments with the pliers, which he laid into her hand.

She lifted the silver pellet between them. Brazen held the magnifier for her without being asked while, with the snips, she opened the pellet along the seam. As she had expected, a curl of parchment wedged inside. She lifted it free and smoothed it open, careful not to touch anything with bare fingers.

Neat and precise in black ink, it contained a drawing of a scarab.

When Bijou snorted, the parchment fluttered. "Of course, you old bastard. It wouldn't be any fun if I didn't know."

Bone scraped bone inside the joints, but her hand was firm as she dropped the parchment and the pellet into another shallow dish and set in place a silver lid that chimed. She lay her tools aside and stood, staring, at her own twisted fingers.

"Bijou?"

She lifted her chin, but didn't manage to drag her gaze any higher than Brazen's chest.

"What do you know?" he asked.

"Funny," she said. "I was just about to ask you the same thing. What do you know?"

"About what?"

It was too much effort holding her head up. "About how the Young Bey's father got to be Bey before him."

"Funny," Brazen echoed. "Not much. You never did like to talk about it."

"Right," she said. "Let me cauterize this wound, and then go and make some tea, and I'll tell you all about it."

He laid a hand upon her wrist. "The *kapikulu* can make your tea tonight, Bijou."

WHEN THE ROOM stank of scorched hair and flesh and the jackal slept in the child's old cage, Brazen and Bijou sat on stools beside the fire together. The child curled on a rug with its back against Bijou's knees. Brazen watched her hands as she spoke, because she had to keep shifting her eyes away from his.

"Before you were born," she said, stroking the child's matted hair, "your father left me for a foreign Sorceress."

"My mother."

Bijou's old face creased. "After a fashion."

A surge of emotion silenced Brazen, almost blinded him. Bijou, he knew, would believe it pity—and find it intolerable. So he did not touch her, even to lay a hand on her shoulder or push back the forbidding snakes of her hair.

He held in a breath while he thought, then said softly, "You were my mother in every manner that mattered."

It was not a lie. She was the only mother that mattered. Any other longing he might feel was only a child's fantasy.

"I did not mean to provoke reassurances," she said, without looking at him. But he saw how her chin lifted, and the small straightening of her spine. "What I meant was that she died before she could birth you. Your mother had the ear of all crawling things, every beast that creeps with its belly to the earth, and that was her power. Her name of craft was Salamander, but I knew her first-name, and she was Wove to me."

Her voice had taken on a sing-song quality, something of a chant such as you might hear of a storyteller from her distant long-forsaken homeland. Brazen did not interrupt her; he dared not, when she was bringing him this gift of memory. But he let his lips move on the word, the name he had never before heard.

Wove.

His mother's name, and a gift of power.

"She named me Michael?" he asked, because it was important to him, suddenly, to know.

Bijou shook her head. "That was your father's choice."

She paused, as if to give him a moment to collect himself, and now she turned her head to look at him directly. When his focus returned to her, she again looked down and spoke.

"We were adventurers, Brazen. Salamander and Kaulas and the Old Bey, who was but Prince Salih in those days. We fought in the name of the old Old Bey, for it was not expected that Prince Salih would inherit his father's title. He was a younger son, you see."

Her pause might have been to gather her thoughts, but Brazen felt the need to fill it. "I did not know that. I mean, I knew there had been a quarrel when the Old Bey came to power, because the old Old Bey's advisors in their wisdom chose to pass over Prince Salih's brother and give the title to Prince Salih. But I did not know—"

"It was our quarrel," Bijou said.

This time, Brazen left the silence empty.

She filled it, after a time. "Salamander and Kaulas and I stood with the Old Bey against his brother. Kaulas had spurned me to pursue Salamander, but she and I were sisters-of-decision and we had agreed that he would not come between us. When the Old Bey's brother came against us, she was swollen with Kaulas' child—with you, Brazen."

"Were you not angry?" he asked.

She managed to hold his gaze when she looked up again. "Wove and I had decided to raise the child together."

Brazen's heart shivered in his chest like a watch gear. "That's not what happened."

"She died," Bijou said. "She died, and Kaulas—he arranged things. So that you could be carried to term. Or near enough."

"Vajhir," Brazen breathed. "Kaulas the Necromancer. No, he never told me. How..."

"How did he do it?"

"How long?"

"Eight weeks," Bijou said. "I stayed with her."

Brazen wanted to ask, as if in asking he could force her to deny the implications of what she said. As if he could rewrite history and make it somehow less terrible. "She knew what had happened?"

Bijou smiled. "She knew she was dead. But she gave you life, my dear, and named you. She named you *Harun*. It was your first name, and your true name, and your father never knew it. And when you had eight years, you came to live with me."

She reached out and patted his hand with her dry, horny one. "I know why he's chosen now. It's because he and I are dying. And he's not the sort to let nature take its course."

"You think he's using what he takes from his abominations to feed his own strength."

"It's the obvious thaumaturgy, isn't it?" She gestured to the covered dishes of putrescence still set on her workbench.

"It is traditional for wizards to struggle mightily once their time approaches. And I admit, I don't like dying very much myself. But I look forward to Death herself, once the dying is over."

"So how do we answer?"

Bijou smiled. "We bring the fight into the street. Unless you have a better plan?"

She looked at Brazen. Brazen shrugged helplessly.

"Then we do it my way," she said.

He squeezed her hand. "When this is over, I want you and the child to come and stay with me."

"But darling," Bijou answered. "Where would I keep the elephant?"

WHILE THE OTHER bone and jewel creatures, even down to the scuttling crab-carapaces, dispersed upon the errand Bijou set them, Hawti helped Brazen tote another procession of chests and crates from his carriage.

And Bijou arrayed herself for war. She bound her hair back with jeweled scarabs which sunk their legs deep in the snaky locks, and she garbed herself in trousers and coat like a man. When she had been young and dressed as a boy, men had stared. Now, her waist bulged rather than nipping in; her buttocks were more like saddlebags than peaches. It didn't matter; Brazen wasn't a man to her, any more than he had given any indication that he thought of her as a woman.

For which mercy she thanked Iashti, the patron of spring and increase, profusely—even if Iashti was not her particular goddess, or one that Bijou had ever found much use for.

She had hoped it might be some hours before her creatures returned, but it was not to be. The crabs first, dragging a struggling, stinking pigeon between them, which Bijou had to net because she did not care to touch it. However much it fought, the bird was long-dead, and Bijou set it to boil.

The silver mackerel-tabby alley cat Ambrosias returned with was not so lucky. Or perhaps luckier, as it was still alive when Bijou got to it, though both of its forepaws were nearly skeletonized. "Hideous," Brazen said, but Bijou only scratched beneath its chin while he fetched her scalpels.

It purred for her. "Who's a sweet puss?" she said. It rubbed its cheek against her fingers.

Brazen shook his head. "You are a strange woman."

"It's not the cat's fault. Come hold it down."

BRAZEN WATCHED HER work, and wished there were some way he could save her. The drag of exhaustion came in the first hours. As the work milled on, her hands—so firm—began to tremble. Brazen built an elevating stool for her so she could sit by her table rather than standing, and while she performed her surgeries, he was the one who wired and soldered and made tiny delicate armatures. They were not, of course, the armatures that Bijou would have constructed—hers, for one thing, would not have been built around minuscule hydraulics and infinitesimal pistons, but Brazen did not build with living things—but she did not seem unpleased by them. She reached up to pat his shoulder, rather, and grinned bravely when he showed her how they articulated.

The smile wore hard. As if it pinched her cheeks. He imagined if she didn't prop her face up with it she might crumble. Fingers moved gently along the incomplete, pipestem-thin brass tubes of the cats-paws until she found a place where the pressure of her thumb made the paw flex wide, and razor-fine steel talons slide from oiled sheaths.

Reverently, Bijou laid the prosthesis on the bench again. Brazen pretended not to see how heavily she leaned against it, her arms bent at the elbows. "What are we going to do with them all? There's too many."

He looked at her, and did her the dignity of not saying, *You can't do it alone.* "A little rest," he said.

"There's too much work." Once she would have done it, too. He imagined her, in the privacy of her own head, cursing the swelling feet, the knotted hands, the age that slowed her. She had been an indomitable force of his childhood, his apprenticeship, and the rock he had leaned upon when he eventually broke away from Kaulas. He'd come to her first, to learn what he needed to know before he struck out on his own. With what she had told him, he could imagine how much it had cost her to treat him gently, as a beloved child. And if her rage seeped out occasionally—he had always known it was aimed at his father, and not at him at all.

"A little rest," he said. "And let me send for my students."

The arch of her eyebrows said it all, and the way the lines drew down on either side of her turtle-beak nose. "You don't think I can manage."

"I don't think *I* can manage." He laid a hand on her arm. "Bijou, sit. Rest. If you make yourself sick fighting him, he's still won."

Sick wasn't what he meant, exactly, and he knew she knew it. But she frowned and sat. Sulkily, like a reprimanded child, with her arms crossed over her chest so her knobby, knitted sleeves draped lumpily from her wrists.

"The feral child has better manners," Brazen said, gesturing to where it curled in the hearth-corner, near the cage in which its injured packmate lay breathing slow and raggedly. Under and behind the cage and bed—in the niche beside the fire and against the wall near the door to the side garden—crouched the wary shadows of the other jackals.

They were not happy, by their pricked ears and watchful eyes. But they were also not leaving.

And they had not turned aside from the food Brazen had caused to be brought for them, especially once they had seen how enthusiastically the child applied itself to the platters of grains and kitfo.

"Better manners?" Bijou glared, but could not sustain it. Her frown cracked into a reluctant smile.

He said, "Someday, when it's a Wizard too, it can be crabby."

"So is it to be your apprentice, then?"

He shrugged. "Who knows what it wants? Can you apprentice a child that can't speak?"

"Can you fail to?" Bijou's smile fell away. "But we were talking about your other apprentices."

Brazen tipped his head. "Some of them are journeymen."

"Whatever they are. Fetch your damned students, and let them overrun my home if that's what makes you happy."

"Actually," Brazen said, "I thought we'd send the work to them. What's the point in having an automatic carriage if I don't put it to use? Bijou..."

She turned away, towards the open garden door. In the courtyard, Catherine settled, wings mantling whatever unfortunate creature dangled from its talons. "I'm listening," Bijou said, pushing herself up against the table edge.

"He can keep making monsters," Brazen said, frustrated. "But what we're doing is as useless as building walls against encroaching dunes. Until we take control of the war, we are losing. And then there's the question of what we are going to do with all the—" He gestured around the room, to the wounded animals, the half-assembled armatures of bone and metal and stone laid out on benches like so many blacksmith's puzzles.

"Turn them loose," Bijou said. "And wait for people to bring us more."

Six

THE CUB HAS come to an understanding.

At first, the brothers-and-sisters are uncertain of their place here. The mother, in particular, fears for her cubs—but she can smell that the cub, who was sick unto dying, is sick no longer. And she can smell it as well, when the father begins to recover, and lift his head inside the bars of the cage.

When the father's flank has sealed, and puffy proud flesh shows where soft speckled coat grew, when he has risen and begun to pace his cage, limping and staggering and dull-coated but hungry and determined—then the old creature comes and slides part of the bars of the cage aside.

The mother's ears come up, her eyes forward. Around her, the brothers-and-sisters lie or crouch or turn tensely, lips tight with worry across closed teeth, tails low slung or quivering just at the tip.

It could be a trap. The men are known for the traps they set, and some are very clever.

The father hesitates. He has crowded to the corner of the cage, furthest from where the old creature stands. Now, as she backs away—slowly, and with the dragging gait of the hip-lame—the father comes forward, hesitation-step, only to pause with one forepaw lifted just inside the cage. The threshold dares him; he lowers his head and flattens his ears.

The cub sidles forward, out of range of the mother's teeth. She might warn it back, and it knows the doorway is safe. The cub has crossed it many times.

The cub leaps up, lightly, beside the father, who tilts his head at it. And then it leaps down, and the father follows, staggering a little when his weight hits weakened forelegs. But the cub is there to steady him. There is a static moment when the father wavers and the mother and the brothers-and-sisters lean forward, held back as if by chains and collars. Then their reserve snaps and the pack surges forward, sniffing and wriggling and surrounding the father until the cub has to put its bone and jewel arm around him and hold him up against the onslaught of relief and congratulations.

And the mother, though the cub does not think the old creature hears the thanks in it, lifts her head to stare at the old creature and fans her tail once, gently.

When dusk comes, the cub shows the pack some of the things it has learned. Such as where the den of the enemy is. Though anyone could tell it for its stinking.

DAYS PASSED, AND the stream of afflicted grew. In the mornings, at first light, Bijou would shuffle from her bedroom to find one of the door-warders had already set water to boil for coffee. She would stir the porridge—sometimes she had to pull the spoon from a servant's hand to do so—and stump to the front door, the child by now usually beside her, and perhaps a jackal as well. When Bijou opened the portal, the cold morning would greet her—and, shivering upon the street before her house, a line of men and women: some with livestock, some with loved ones, some hunched over their own necrotizing injuries.

Bijou would treat them as best she could, the ones that were within saving. The ones that were not within saving could not be allowed to go free. But Brazen took responsibility for those; he went before the Bey and prevailed upon him to open the jails as quarantine, which the Bey could do without involving his advisors. There, those that died and would not lie down could be kept in custody.

This did not prevent some from dying untreated, of course, and soon Messaline fluttered with stinking pigeons and swarmed with necrotic rats. The river fouled and only covered cisterns stayed safe for drinking—though some must, perforce, drink the river water or go thirsty. And still Bijou's bone and jewel creatures brought her more and more of the dead and dying.

Bijou's unquiet loft hummed with people—the comings and goings of Brazen's household, the child's jackal wardens like ghosts about the garden, the sick. And, more and more, it was also busy with the recovering. Once healing had begun, many of those returned to assist with the still-sick. Lazybones hid in the attics so that Bijou hardly even heard it. The street before Bijou's house, and for yards in every direction, took on the aspect of a fair.

The first treated animal to be released was the cat, new forelimbs silenced cunningly with tiny leather pads upon the toes. Bijou carried it to the back garden wall and set it down, stroking its ears when it twined her ankles. "Go on," she said. "Be about your business."

As if the work she and Brazen had put into it and its brethren had made them, like her Artifices, capable of understanding her speech, the cat looked at her, meowed condescendingly, looked away again, and with a smooth leap mounted the garden wall.

Two hours later, it returned with the neck of a fluttering undead pigeon gripped in its teeth, the bird shedding gobs of putrescence and pecking at its eyes.

"Oh thank you," Bijou said. "Just what I wanted."

As she lurched forward, Brazen burst from her loft, a parchment fluttering from his fingers like a fan. By its freight of ribbons and wax, she knew the source even before he called, "Bijou! I am summoned to speak before the Bey!"

BRAZEN WENT ALONE, on foot, so as to seem humble. He went with the dawnlight, Iashti's time, for a good beginning. He went in sandals and plain robes, so as to seem scholarly, but though his turban was coarse black cloth, still he wound it seven times. And having wound it, and made his sash tight, he also divested himself of all weapons.

When he presented himself before the *kapikulu* guarding the Bey's gates, they searched him as carefully as he had anticipated, but they did not demand his letter of invitation before allowing him passage. It served as a small reassurance that his star had not yet fallen irretrievably.

Such things could change very fast, when it came to politics. But it seemed that they had not changed *yet*.

The Young Bey sat upon a gilt platform amid silken rugs and mirrored cushions, a tray resting at his right hand upon a low cradle. *Kapikulu* stood like skirted statues at every corner of the room, their coats as stark as the marble floor.

Aware of their gaze, and the attention of the Young Bey, Brazen lowered himself to the stones, swished the skirts of his linen robes out from under his knees, and crept forward. He thought of the jackal-child as he slid his palms across cold marble, tracing pewter-and-black veins. When his fingertips touched the edge of the platform, he paused and touched the floor with the peak of his turban.

"Your excellence," he said. "Your unworthy servant begs your indulgence."

"Face me," the Bey said. Brazen pushed himself back onto his suffering knees.

"At your command," he said, so the Bey rolled his eyes at him.

"Come, sit," the Bey said. "And pour the coffee. Let us set aside formalities today, Brazen, and be men who were once teacher and student."

Though he called himself a man, the Bey's hands were as smooth as his cheeks, or the silken pillows he rested his backside on. Those hands lay upon his knees as Brazen edged up the stairs, careful never to turn his back. He sat one step below the Bey, off the cushions, and reached to pour two tiny cups of tarry coffee. The smell rising with steam from the cups was so rich and bitter it made his eyes water. There were sweets also, layered heaps of nuts and honey and threads of pastry.

Brazen served two to the Bey and chose one for himself, lifting it on a cloth napkin once the Bey had taken a bite of his own. This was a gesture of great trust, and a subtle message. The Bey had spoken as if man to man, and taken food from his hand. This conversation was not one of a subject to his ruler, but rather one between two acquaintances.

That also implied that the Bey did not anticipate that he would be able to offer any assistance, which did not surprise Brazen at all. But first there were pleasantries to be dispensed with, and so they were. And there was coffee to be sipped, and so it was.

And finally the Bey leaned down close to Brazen's ear and spoke softly, for his hearing alone. "You have come to beg assistance against Kaulas the Necromancer."

"It is a formality," Brazen said.

"My advisors will not hear of interfering in a Wizard war."

"That is as I told my old master," Brazen said. "Also, that Kaulas set your father in his place, and when in that service he placed the Council, he placed men loyal to himself."

The Bey sat back, a grim smile twisting his lips. "So you will understand when I tell you that I cannot give you men, or any succor or comfort when you brace him."

"I will understand many things," Brazen agreed. He bit down on pastry, though it might as well have been a swallow's nest for all the pleasure it gave him. Brushing crumbs from his beard gave him a moment to school his expression. "I understand that a man faces many difficulties in life, and he cannot always choose how he meets them."

"It is true," the Bey said. "True and yet a source of sorrow for all devout men. Still, a great service may be remembered with gratitude."

"Indeed," said Brazen. "Or disquiet, in gratitude's failure."

BIJOU KNEW FROM Brazen's stride, from the swirl of his robes about his ankles and the way his sandals hit the floor, that the conversation with the Bey had gone no better than anticipated. But because it was expected, she laid down her corruption-soaked tools and stepped back from the current cadaver, holding fouled hands wide. "Well?" she said.

Brazen's sigh was gusty enough that Bijou half-thought she should feel it across the loft. He broke his stride and folded his arms, choosing to stand well back from her work table.

"He says that if we kill Kaulas for him, he'll try not to hold the favor against us."

"Oh," Bijou said.

Brazen nodded. "Yes. That went about as well as I expected. So what now?"

Bijou nodded to the deliquescing carcass pinned before her. "We chase Kaulas from his den, my dear one."

MAYBE NOW THE old creature trusts the cub to return. At least, she has made the new-creatures—the ones that carry scimitars and stand as still as doors—allow the cub and the mother and the brothers-and-sisters to come and go as they please. And where they please to come and go is to and from the stinking den of the enemy.

The cub—and the mother—understand now that the old creature and her allies are pack, or at least they are pack as one might find pack in the dry season, when the lions are lean and will hunt even jackals, if they can get them. So they do what jackals do best, and at the edge of the enemy's territory ghost from crevice to shadow, waiting for what he will do.

The cub is most tireless of the sentries, along with the mother. The mother seems to have chosen it, to rely upon its judgment now as she did not before, and this makes the cub lift its chest with pride. If the cub had a ruff and proper ears, they would be puffed up.

Instead, it leans its shoulder on the mother's shoulder as they crouch in the shadow of a vine-hung wall out of eyeshot of the enemy's den, but within range by even the cub's crippled sense of smell. The cub presses its face under her neck in submission and gratitude. The mother—warm, richly scented and soft—stretches her neck and turns her head, returning the caress. And then they wait, and try to avoid the notice of the occasional vicious dead things that shamble or flutter through increasingly-deserted streets.

And wait some more, through lingering evenings and still-sharp days.

It so happens that when the enemy at last emerges from his den, the cub and the mother are crouched under that very arbor. The enemy comes forth on the last day of autumn, which falls exactly between the equinox and the solstice, in the grey light before the sun breaks over the horizon and begins sending its red fingers seeking between the walls of Messaline. On another day, the markets would be bustling in the morning cool, but some premonition must have stolen into the stall-keepers in their beds. Because the progress of the enemy's reeking army through the streets is met by silence, barred doors and vacant streets, and heralded only by the stench of corpses and the long strides of jackals running before him.

BIJOU HAD NEVER heard the city jackals howl before. Certainly the jackals of the river, the ones she knew from her childhood, were anything but silent, so she knew they must be able to yip and cry and converse. But the jackals who lived within Messaline were next to ghosts, silent as shadows. So to hear their concerted cries in the street jerked her upright in her bed. Beyond the alcove curtain, Hawti rang like a carnival as it strode towards the door.

Bijou groped for her spectacles, balancing them on her nose while struggling her feet to the floor.

She did not need to ask. She stood, rocking to her feet—perhaps the urgency of crisis was not a panacea after all. The previous day's robes hung over her vanity stool. She shrugged them on, thrusting buttons through holes with an aching thumb, and faced herself in her mirror, where she made her face stern and empty.

Of course, he had waited for Kaalha's season to pass, and Vajhir's to begin. At least it was winter and not the killing summer. But he must have begun his campaign then.

Bijou stared at herself sternly in the mirror, and tucked her hammer in her sash before she went out to face the Necromancer, brushing past the *kapikulu* at her front door as if they were no more than cords of hanging coins and crystals.

KAULAS CAME WITH her bone raven on his shoulder, as if to prove that she could wrest from him nothing that he could not take back. But she had Brazen at her side to give the lie, and jackals glared green-eyes from every shadow. Kaulas walked, his gait crisp and unhurried, and Bijou stood with her gnarled hands on her gnarled stick and watched him walk—tall and stern and as spry as if he were not easily as old as she—at the head of his army of the dead, all of them filling up the broad boulevard that led to her front door.

Bijou had something of an army behind her, as well. Brazen and his men-at-arms and his mechanicals at her left hand. The child and the jackals at her right. Her creatures arrayed behind her—the ones she had made over years past from relicts and mementos mori, and the new ones who were still-living, salvaged from Kaulas' creeping necrosis. Ambrosius clattered at her feet, and just behind her Lazybones dragged itself over the cobblestones with a rowing motion, scratching the mirrors on its belly but determined not to be left behind.

"Kaulas," she said, when she thought he was close enough to hear her. He was certainly close enough for the stench to carry.

He came a few strides closer before he halted, as if to prove she could not make him hesitate. No surprise there, she thought. She never could.

The jeweled insect brooches in her hair danced in anticipation. "Kaulas," she said again. "Don't pretend that you can't hear me."

In defiance of the desert, Kaulas wore black: a flapping-tailed northern coat and trousers over a crisp white shirt tied at the collar in a bow. Bijou looked at his hard-planed cheeks, the sagging line of what had been a beautiful jaw. She had had one of her own, once upon a time. She might have lifted a hand to brush her wattled throat, but she would not give Kaulas the satisfaction of seeing her fidget.

"Well," she said, "You have my attention. For once. What did you plan to do with it?"

"Keep it," he said.

One bony hand made an elegant gesture, and something came forward from the press of animate dead behind him. A woman, Bijou thought at first. Though she came walking slowly, veiled as if against the desert dust and heat, Bijou knew her walk. Though it had been a sorcerer's lifetime since Bijou bid her farewell, she knew the tilt of her head.

"I destroyed that," Bijou said, as the corpse of a woman once named Wove paused beside Kaulas and lifted her veil from her moth-pale hair. "I *destroyed* that."

"I certainly let you think so," Kaulas said. He turned his face away as if he were shutting a door. "Brazen, won't you come meet your mother, my son?"

He moved, of course. How could he not? She was beautiful as the day she died, her face waxen, expressionless under the powder that loaned it a semblance of the glow of life. She stared at Bijou through clouded eyes, lashes half-lowered, and Brazen first took two steps back and then, as if unwilling, one forward.

And then another.

His jaw worked. His voice creaked as he never would have permitted one of his constructs to creak. "Let her go," he said. "You may own everything else in Messaline, old man. But don't think you're going to own *me* that way."

Kaulas rubbed left fingers against his palm as if assessing a handful of soil. When he looked up from the gesture, he smiled a little, self-deprecating. "Come here and I'll let her go."

"Don't do it," Bijou said. She cracked the ferrule of her cane against the stones and Brazen's head finally turned, though she wasn't sure his eyes focused on her. His expression was terrible with yearning and rage.

"Brazen," Bijou said, and prayed not to the gods but to Wove that Wove, on behalf of her son, would forgive her. "She's just bait. She's just one of his dead things. That's not her, she doesn't know what he's done to her."

Brazen smiled. "You told me the truth already, Bijou." When he had spoken, he did not turn away, but kept his eyes on her face. Bijou reached to clutch his sleeve. As if she were nothing, he moved one more step towards Kaulas, using the arm she was not clutching to gesture his *kapikulu* back.

"Wove," Brazen said. He still did not take his eyes off Bijou. "What was it that you named me, before I took the name Brazen?"

Bijou heard the fibers of his sleeve snap under her fingernails. She felt a held breath still in him, and looked up to see Wove turn her head to stare at Kaulas, waiting his command.

"Brazen," Bijou said, "he is only trying to own you."

"I know what I'm doing," Brazen whispered. Bijou shook her head. How could he?

"Answer your son, my dear," Kaulas said.

Her voice might have been huskier than when she was alive, or—just as easily—it could be Bijou's recollection that was at fault. It was, however, still fluid and musical. The difference was that the Wove Bijou remembered was not grateful to receive orders.

"I named you Harun," she said. "I only told your name to Bijou."

"You're her," Brazen said, and shook Bijou's hand from his arm as he started forward.

Bijou knew the set of his shoulders. No argument would call him back now, from whatever he was planning.

So she pulled the hammer from her sash and hurled it full in Kaulas' face.

He ducked aside. He must have been expecting it—oh, they knew each other well, the woman whose name meant *Jewel* and the man whose name meant *Ashes*—and her hammer sailed past him to vanish among the dead. But all she needed was the moment's break in his concentration.

Lucy surged forward to catch Brazen up and drag him back behind the line. He kicked, but it lifted him by the elbows and swung him clear, his striped caftan swirling about his ankles. Bijou feared that he would set his constructs on her Artifices, or that the *kapikulu* would hack at Lucy, who Bijou could not allow to defend herself. But Brazen yelled them back between curses—"We cannot fight amongst ourselves!"—then turned his wrath on Bijou.

"Damn you," he yelled. "Did you think me ensorceled?"

Kaulas lifted up one gloved hand and sent his dead things forward.

It was a matter of instants for the faceoff to become a skirmish and for Brazen's invective to become protectiveness. He grabbed Bijou's elbow as the bone and jewel creatures hurled themselves forward, flanked by the jackals and Brazen's hissing constructs and the whirling *kapikulu* like a storm of skirted coats and swords. The *kapikulu* shrieked like a rising wind and the artifices rang with bells and clattered like marionettes or whistled and clanked and hissed with steam, but the dead and the jackals made no sound at all.

The street flowed with rot and blood, with machine oil and scalding water. Bijou kept her head down, stumping backwards on her cane, letting Hawti come before her as a shield. She lost track of the others—here, Catherine's ragged wings; there, Ambrosius clotted with gelled blood— and now Brazen seemed done with fighting Lucy. The gorilla looked at Bijou for instruction.

"Put him down," Bijou said, and when that was finished she motioned Lucy into the fray, though she winced to do it. She heard the clash of metal and bone. Somewhere out there, the dead were armed. And somewhere out there, her Artifices were wounded.

She leaned on Brazen's arm, gasping, and let him drag her into an eddy behind the combat. Before them, Hawti rattled its trunk and waded forward, laying about itself with tusks and feet. Bijou saw it totter, saw it rock and tumble sideways as the dead pulled it down. She saw limbs and gore hurled as it thrashed, rending the rotting enemy even as they levered up cobbles with which to smash its bones.

"Emeraude," Bijou said, realizing the child had slipped forward into the fight. "Emeraude!"

Now it was Brazen's turn to pull *her* aside. Something big rattled past them, brass and iron, thick fluid leaking from every joint. She kicked him sharply in the shins; he lifted her up on tiptoe and pushed her back against the wall. "Bijou, dammit—"

"The *child*," she said, and he turned to search over his shoulder.

"I don't—"

Kaulas' voice boomed out of the fight like a cavalry trumpet. "Bijou, call off your dogs or your little rat dies!"

She would never know how she broke free of Brazen. Panic strength, and it didn't matter that he was protecting her. She left rags of cloth clenched in his fingers as she staggered past him, plunging into the thick of the fight, shouting already. "Let it go, Kaulas, or I swear I'll shoe it in your *guts*."

THERE'S A KNIFE at the cub's neck, sharp enough to freeze it in place instinctively. It knows if it twists, the blade will cut it. It knows if it fights, the enemy will slash its throat.

And so it hangs in his grip and pretends to be helpless, and waits for its moment.

Not too far off, the father crouches over the mother's body, and the mother does not move. The cub feels that like a bee sting inside it whenever it lets its eyes roll that way, but the bee sting hurts and distracts it, so instead it pins its gaze on the face of the enemy. It's a man, just an old man with a raven skeleton on its shoulder, and it's not even looking at the cub, or the father, or anything. It looks past the father, at something the cub can't turn its head far enough to see.

But the cub can hear it. Spitting like a caged lioness, lurching across uneven stones as if its weary feet never slowed it, the old creature charges into view. It checks the length of a short leap from the enemy and pauses there, still as stone.

It snarls and the enemy makes some noise back that should sound like pleading but isn't, it's gloating. The other creature, the loud one with the garish colors, appears behind the old creature and grabs its black sleeve. The old creature makes a soft brief noise, though, and the loud one puffs up like it took a big breath and then lets go again as it deflates.

The father growls low in his throat when the enemy turns towards him. The mother does not move. The cub must—really must—stop looking.

The cub looks at the old creature instead.

The old creature makes noises, and the enemy makes noises back. Then there is a rain of clicks and chimes, as bone creatures shed from the old one's hair and clothing— small things, no bigger than a thumb, like beetles. They ring like coins as they fall.

When they are done falling, the old creature comes forward. The loud one reaches after it, but it moves beyond reach of the loud creature's fingertips with a graceful sway, a sidestep that belongs to a much younger animal.

And then it comes up beside the enemy, and the enemy lets the cub slip from its grasp.

The cub scrambles back, back, until it feels the mother's fur and slack warm body brush its feet. It crouches beside the father, shivering with wrath and fear, and noses the mother.

The scent that fills its awareness is not the scent of anything alive, and the father shakes, crouching, teeth bared in a display the cub cannot match. No matter how desperately it wishes.

And now the old creature stands before the enemy, the enemy's fist knotted in the snakes of its pelt. The enemy reaches up with the knife and presses it beneath the old creature's chin. The old creature closes its eyes, but not before—

Not before the cub sees it look across a gap of space at the loud creature and—for an instant—close just a single eye.

The enemy makes a sound. A short sharp bark of a sound. And sways into the motion of the knife.

MINE, KAULAS SAID, and Bijou felt the blade prick her throat, part flesh, glide along her skin like a caress. But the child was free, beyond Kaulas' reach. And Bijou was not about to let Kaulas claim her as he had claimed Wove, and then inevitably Brazen. Death was no escape from a necromancer.

Aladdin the raven watched her from Kaulas' shoulder, turning so the light gleamed through his blue, flawed eye. If she could reach him—touch him—

—she did not think Kaulas could keep him from her, if she were close enough to touch. But Kaulas was taller, long-limbed, and the knife held her at a distance. Even when her creatures dragged themselves up around him— she heard the rattle of Ambrosius's legs, syncopated now that so many were broken, and the slow slow scrape of glass on stone as Lazybones hauled itself over slimed cobbles—they would not come closer while he threatened their mistress.

But that was as it should be. And the lady of death was the lady of moths, also.

"All this just to *own* us?" Bijou said, as slow blood rolled down her throat. "So be it. You'll own nothing again."

She stepped forward onto the knife, and as she did, she raised her right hand and brushed the wing of the bone raven sitting like a trophy on Kaulas' shoulder. "Aladdin," she said. "I free you."

The rest of her incantation died on the knife. But she had spoken her intent, and with her blood and breath across the bird's skull that was what mattered.

BRAZEN SAW HER hurl herself onto the knife. He saw her hand rise. He saw the palm slide down the bones of the animate bird skeleton. He saw the mirror-sharp skeleton of the sloth shuffle forward from the edge of the ring of watching creatures to rise up behind the Necromancer and drag hooked claws as long as human fingers though his hamstrings and across his lower back, drive them through flesh and twist.

He saw the raven turn, open its beak, and sink the beveled steel point of its hypodermic tongue into the angle where Kaulas' jaw joined his throat, silencing him before he could speak a dying spell.

Neither one of them screamed.

But the Necromancer tried to.

BIJOU—

Oh, Bijou.

She lay in blood that first bubbled and then seeped and then stopped, and Brazen could do nothing to staunch it. The knowledge did nothing to prevent him from reddening his hands in the attempt.

Despite anything he tried, she went quickly, the raven perched beside her on the stones, the sloth rocking worriedly beside her. When her breath had stilled and the blood stuck to his fingers rather than seeping across them, only then did he whisper, "You should have let me take care of it."

But then, he wasn't sure after all that he would have been able to.

Brazen leaned back on his heels and looked up.

The first thing he saw was the child, crouched over one dead jackal, flank to flank with a scarred and living one. The next was the raven, wings still half-spread, cocking its one-eyed head from side to side. Still animate. Still moving.

Brazen turned on his toes without rising from his crouch. They had come up around him, Kaulas' creatures and Brazen's and Bijou's, the animate dead and the animate machines and the jeweled skeletons, many crushed and torn and missing pieces. They stood and waited, and did not judge—or if they judged, they did so silently.

As silently as the child, who had not moved from its place beside its packmates. Other jackals slung from amid the crowd to lurk beside them, shadows on the slick and stinking stones. He wondered if the corpse of his mother was still among them.

He thought he could find out later. And find out, too, if she still wished to be destroyed. It was a decision for another day, one which did not already hold so many terrible decisions.

"You'll all come home with me," Brazen said, looking from the re-animated to the living to the never-living at all.

The child looked up at Brazen with eyes gone huge as he rose to his feet. Whether his words meant anything to it, he did not know. But it straightened up, holding itself like a young person rather than a wild animal, and touched his hand with the fingertips of its bone and jewel one. It looked over its shoulder, where the pack had gathered around the corpse of one of their own, and made a yearning gesture.

"I can't," he said. "I'm sorry."

It shuddered all over. Brazen touched its hair. He thought the gesture would send it haring away, but it suffered the caress. Afterwards, it withdrew just beyond the length of his arm and stared up at him.

It did not shy away, though, when the captain of the *kapikulu* came up through the ranks of the dead.

"Enchanter," he said. "What are your instructions?"

He took a breath. Faces were appearing in windows and the corners of doorways. There was a public face to be put on this. And a hero to be remembered.

"Lash your spears to carry the Wizard Bijou," Brazen said. "She must be honored. Bring her to Kaalha's House. I will await you."

But it turned out he couldn't leave while they were seeing to Bijou, because he could not walk away from her. And nor would Emeraude, who flitted back and forth between Bijou's corpse and that of the she-jackal, touching each with featherlight gestures, clawed fingers that scrabbled as if to clutch, but never quite locked on what they touched.

When the remaining *kapikulu* lifted Bijou's body, Brazen found himself beside the child. It gentled the he-jackal as Brazen lifted the female in his arms. She weighed no more than seed-puff, a fistful of feathers. So burdened, it seemed only right that he fell in behind Bijou's bier rather than leading the way, as had been his intent.

It was fitting that he should walk this last mile with Bijou. As her guard of honor. And it was fitting that he should carry the jackal who had come to fight beside them, though Kaulas' wrath had only slopped over onto her pack by accident.

Before they started forward, however, the captain of the *kapikulu* stepped before Brazen, straightening his gore-soaked coat. "And the Necromancer?"

Brazen turned away. "Leave him for the jackals," he said, and then paused and looked back over his shoulder. "You know what? Actually, you'd better take his head."

"Just in case," the captain said. "And burn it?"

"Just in case." Brazen smiled a smile that made his cheeks burn. "He *was* the Necromancer. I'd hate to take any chances."

THE CUB FOLLOWS the loud creature and the loud creature follows the old creature's body, which the men in long coats carry with as much gentleness as if she is only sleeping and they do not wish to wake her. She is not sleeping. The cub can smell the death on her.

The cub wants to howl, but its throat tightens around the sound it would like to make. So it walks silently, the father and the brothers-and-sisters close beside it. They will not leave the cub—or the mother.

Not yet.

They do not go to any place the cub has been before. It might worry at being out of its territory, but the pack is there—all of its packs, both packs—and it is too tired and sad to be afraid. It is almost too tired and sad to walk, but everyone else is walking, and the cub won't be left behind.

Even the mirrored creature creeps along behind, scraping itself along the stones until the big broad bone creature with the hands stops and picks it up, slinging it from its chest like an infant. That comforts the cub. The cub does not think it could stand to see anyone else left behind.

They come to a building—a man den—bigger even than the enemy's den, and the cub thinks they will stop outside it. But instead the bearers lead them up a broad shallow set of steps and into a den built of silver-and-black stones, under a portico hung with silk awnings and strings of flashing mirrors.

A rank of robed creatures meet them here, and at first the cub flinches from them. They are men, male and female, and each of them wears a mirrored mask split down the middle with a jagged line. But they part into welcoming lines to let the procession pass, and when the cub smells them they smell like simple grains and milk, like soap and dates and honey. No blood and no wrath.

As the procession passes between them, they each raise both hands to the separate halves of their masks, as if to remove them, or as if to shield their eyes from horror.

Inside the building is cool, a great echoing space of polished floors with a table at the far end on a raised platform. The table is simple wood, freshly scrubbed, and the source of the good smells. It holds bowls of cooling porridge and honey, glasses of wine.

A man stands in front of it. She wears a gleaming mirrored mask like the others, but her robes are sewn with mirrors and her sleeves of plain white linen drip from arms spread wide. She makes a greeting noise, and sweeps down the steps from the platform.

Something occurs between her and the loud creature, some conversation the cub cannot follow. She strokes the mother's bloody ear and bows her head, which looks like sadness despite the mirrors. With gestures, she points the loud creature and the bearers to lay their burdens before the table.

And then she turns to the cub, and to the pack. She crouches before them, holds out her hand to the father. He cringes and shies back, then creeps forward on tiptoe, coat bristling, to sniff offered fingers at the full stretch of his neck. The cub does not shy so much, but neither does it lean in to sniff.

The robed man stands, and the cub realizes that everyone else has drawn back in a wide ring. It glances over its shoulder, but the path to the door is not blocked. And they must have been careful to leave it open, when there are so many.

The robed man comes forward hesitantly and the cub waits. It lets her touch its ears. It lets her touch its tongue, fingers damp with something that tastes of salt and water, although it makes a face and shakes its head, after.

The robed man draws back, sweeping everything aside with gestures like a pack-mother's, and when it returns it carries bowls of cooling porridge from the altar in its hands. It sets them on the ground before the father and before the cub, then goes back for more, until there are bowls of food or milk or honey before every member of the pack.

Cautiously, the cub inches forward. It crouches, its elbows resting on its knees. And it watches the food and the robed man. But it does not eat, and neither does the father.

WHEN THE EIDOLON of Kaalha backed away from the food she had set with her own hands before the child and its jackal friends, Brazen went forward. She sighed as he came up beside her, so he knew she'd registered his presence, but she did not turn her mirrored mask to face him until he spoke.

"Jackals are sacred to Kaalha," he said.

She looked up. "Jackals are welcome here. But one of those is not a jackal."

"Nor yet is it a human child." Brazen glanced aside. The child had dabbled its jeweled fingers in the bowl before it and was studying the porridge clinging to them, as if readying itself to taste. "I will apprentice it. But—" He looked back at the Eidolon, helplessly. "As we have seen today, even Wizards must return to Kaalha."

While his eyes were on the child, she had raised both hands to her divided mask and pressed one to each side. The reflections of her fingers hovered in the surface. He might be a Wizard of Messaline, but the prospect of the revealed face of a Goddess could still bring a shudder.

Under the mask, one side of her face would be terrible, scarred with acid since her initiation—in homage to the terrible side of the goddess's face. The other—

"You wish me to promise the temple will see to its care when you are gone."

Brazen found himself holding his breath. He forced some of it up his throat, to say, "Yes."

The mask hid all expression. All he could see was her hands, his own worried expression behind them. Of course the child could care for itself. Of course, in the new and ever-stranger Messaline that would grow up from what had changed today.

He had to know, for Bijou's sake, that the child would have safe haven.

She lifted down the left side of her mask, revealing skin blemished only by years and duty, a sparkling black eye framed by an arched brow. Revealed half-lips arched in a half-smile, showing small dry lines around the edges.

"Jackals will always be welcomed here. But Kaalha of the Ruins did not bring you a half-destroyed child for no reason. Now take it home, Brazen the Enchanter, and think of how you will raise it to become a Wizard of Messaline."

Acknowledgements:

I WOULD LIKE TO thank Leah Bobet, Emma Bull, Amanda Downum, Jodi Meadows, Sarah Monette, Jaime Moyer, and Delia Sherman, without whom this would never have been written. I would also like to thank my agent, Jennifer Jackson, who rocks my socks.